Wind

Calvin Miller

Wind

A NOVEL

BETHANYHOUSE
PUBLISHERS
MINNEAPOLIS, MINNESOTA

Wind
Copyright © 2000
Calvin Miller

Cover art: Common Blues by Richard Tratt © Felix Rosenstiel's
Widow and Son Ltd., London.
Photoshop motion blur and barn added by designer.
Cover design by Dan Thornberg

Published by Bethany House Publishers
A Ministry of Bethany Fellowship International
11400 Hampshire Avenue South
Bloomington, Minnesota 55438
www.bethanyhouse.com

Printed in the United States of America by
Bethany Press International, Bloomington, Minnesota 55438

Library of Congress Cataloging-in-Publication Data

Miller, Calvin.
    Wind / by Calvin Miller.
        p.   cm.
    ISBN 0-7642-2362-3
    1. Homeless families—Fiction.   2. Brothers and sisters—Fiction.
3. Pennsylvania—Fiction.   I. Title.
PS3563.I376 W56   2000
813'.54—dc21   00-010472

As with snow,
so with wind,
to Melanie

CALVIN MILLER is a poet, a pastor, a theologian, a painter, and one of Christianity's best-loved writers with over thirty published books. His writing spans a wide spectrum of genres, from the bestselling SINGER TRILOGY to *The Unchained Soul* to the heart-rending novella *Snow*. Miller presently serves as professor of preaching and pastoral ministries at Beeson Divinity School in Alabama, where he and his wife, Barbara, make their home.

1

Peter McCaslin and Ernest Pitovsky had nothing in common except that each—unknown to the other—had inherited the earth at the same time. Both lived where the fortieth meridian crossed the seventy-fifth parallel. Like the cross hairs of a gunsight, those lines drew a bead on King of Prussia, Pennsylvania. The hamlet was small, yet big enough to allow them ample room to exist without ever meeting each other.

If what a person owns defines that person, then the two men's definitions were quite different. Peter owned the dairy just west of King of Prussia, and Ernest owned what he could carry on his back. Peter was married to Kathleen, and Ernest to Helena. Peter had one child; Ernest had two. Peter made a good living on his fine, paid-for farm, and so was sitting as pretty as one might while facing the lean years of the Depression. Such was not the case with Ernest and Helena.

Wall Street failed in October of '29. Ernest was

living in Philadelphia at the time. Though he had nothing invested in the stock market, its crash soon caused his own meager living to crumble. By December he had lost his job as a warehouse man.

Two months later he had lost everything else. This was because Ernest was a man strapped to a large mortgage on a small house. And his wife's illness required that all remaining money be spent on medicine. Shortly after he sold his car—an older model of little value—Ernest and family were evicted from their repossessed home. They now faced the desperate months ahead without any resources.

Completely destitute and with no place to go, Ernest found himself left with but two choices. One was to stay in Philadelphia and try to survive in the city's soup lines and flophouses. But these were often inadequate and degrading. The second option seemed more viable to him: He would move his family out of the city and seek shelter in some vacated building, where they might at least live out of the weather till he could find work again.

Even though Ernest considered this plan a matter-of-fact cure for all his woes, he was dying inside as they headed out of Philadelphia. For he had reduced his family to vagabonds, and it grieved him to think of what he had done to them. A troupe of refugees now, they walked together hoping to escape the hard times.

The heavy snows of December were melted some, though still not completely gone. But the crusted ice proved more difficult to trudge through than the deeper patches of snow. Worst of all, however, were the freezing feet and the long nights. Ernest detested the nights. When the temperature dropped below zero, his self-condemnation rose up. And when he saw his children shivering or crying softly, he immediately turned his gaze inward and scrutinized his shame.

Yet most mornings came wrapped in sunlight, which made the future take on the look of possibility. Ernest felt better when walking in the sun. He carried the important stuff of their survival in a beat-up suitcase and a large bundle. Due to the times, it was very common to meet up with others lugging their own lopsided bundles. Ernest liked greeting them, if only to bring a little courage to his desperation.

In 1930 the American railroads were places of desperation. The tracks acted as arteries for downtrodden people, those who had been driven from a better life. Some who walked the tracks were to be feared, but most were just frightened fugitives like him.

Chief among Ernest's treasures now was a large box of sulfur matches that he kept wrapped in wax paper to keep dry. After five cold nights of sleeping out in the open, they were several miles west of Philadelphia when Ernest discovered a lean-to shack, open on all sides. He enclosed it with leafless branches from some dead brush, breaking up a few of the branches to build a fire. The flames warmed them. He smiled. His two small children appeared to see their pointless pilgrimage now as a kind of adventure. Still, it was an adventure in which they were often hungry.

On the first Sunday morning of February 1930, the Pitovsky family came to a railroad trestle. Beside the rusty span of supports lay a frosted meadow that held an odd collection of junk automobiles. The largest one, though it was missing the seats, had all its windows still intact. *What luck*, Ernest thought. *Solid shelter!* Under the dash of the old car, against what had once been the fire wall, he found a small space that might serve as a fireplace. Ernest then built a tiny fire, arranging it so that the smoke vented safely outside through an opening in the fire wall. He had no intention of remaining there for very long, but considering their penniless condition, he couldn't have asked for anything better. The glowing embers kept them warm, driving out the chilling dampness.

When night came, Ernest watched his children as they rested snugly between him and Helena, listening to her tell them stories. He also kept an eye on their threadbare blankets, to be sure they never came too close to the fire.

Helena seemed cheerful here. But perhaps she felt an obligation to be cheerful simply to encourage Ernest. He bore a continual heaviness that stemmed from his guilt in seeing their finer homelife be replaced by such a makeshift living arrangement. She helped Ernest dream of better things. But all was not well with Helena.

Even as she told the children stories, her speaking was occasionally interrupted by coughing seizures. At times, when her coughing increased in its duration and intensity, Ernest found himself having to turn away to hide the despair he felt. He knew he should do something, but what? There were no jobs, scarcely any means to get food, and they had but a few dollars to buy such basic things as would keep them alive.

Nevertheless, as downcast as Ernest was, he kept reminding himself that he was their best chance for survival.

❧❧❧

The same morning that the Pitovskys had nestled together in the old car, Peter McCaslin and his family took their customary place in one of the pews of St. Olaf's Lutheran Church. Directly after the Episcopal church, St. Olaf's was on the social register of King of Prussia's who's who. The McCaslins always arrived at exactly 10:50 A.M. They needed no clock for this. The time was the result of years of religious habit. As Peter's grandfather had taken his father to church, in like manner Peter's father had taken him.

But punctuality was more than a matter of habit for the McCaslin family; it had become a standard of pride. There were two sins against the Holy Ghost: One was to be late, the other to be ill-dressed. This was the doctrine that Peter's grandfather had asserted as an infallible principle of life.

Dr. Drummond was the Lutheran physician who had delivered Peter's first baby during the December snowstorm two months earlier. He now surveyed the warmly blanketed baby as the McCaslins passed his pew. The nice thing about arriving at ten-fifty was that it allowed a covey of older women to flock about Mrs. Kathleen McCaslin, peel back the bunting, and make a fuss over the newest generation of McCaslins.

With Peter leading the way, they continued walking up the center aisle while being cooed over and pawed at till they finally reached the second pew. The pew had been the religious roost of the McCaslins for over a hundred years. They sat near the front on the right side of the aisle, two pews ahead of the Muellers. Such an arrangement was symbolic for Peter. After all, they out-owned the Muellers and had "discovered" America first.

Peter's mind contained a kind of status meter, which registered the level of importance of those he passed as he made his way to the second pew. Most of the congregation rated low on the meter; however, there were some Peter regarded favorably.

Dr. Drummond of pew seven was one of them, despite Mrs. Drummond's once being a Presbyterian. Of course, like most Scots the McCaslins were

Presbyterian when in the old country, but Peter's great-grandfather had married a German woman three generations before. Since then the McCaslins had all been Lutherans. Indeed, Peter felt that they were such good Lutherans, they could look askew at Mrs. Drummond. For though she had wisely become a Lutheran through marriage, she would always be marked by her Presbyterian birth. Still, Drummond had delivered the McCaslin baby, and his skill as a doctor provided him a place of good standing.

In the fifth pew sat Mabel Cartwright, who, to Peter's way of thinking, was sitting farther forward than she should have been. Mabel was, after all, the village gossip. She owned too little to sit so near the altar. And the stories that went around of her early widowhood were most un-Lutheran. Still, she had always been a Lutheran, although not a very pleasant one.

Mary Withers and Alexis had advanced recently to the fourth pew. Their good fortune had come about at Christmastime, when they became friends with the Muellers. Mary was a poor widow, who had been barely making it since losing her husband. Alexis was sick much of this time. The two of them lived alone then, rarely leaving the house except to go to church. Peter felt sorry for her. *Poor Mary* was how Peter thought of her, and she was always accompanied by *poor Alexis*. Just seeing her caused him to thank God that his family had always been healthier and more blessed.

Yet Peter ranked Mary as having stepped up now because of her obvious close relationship with Erick—the coal boy turned professor. Peter felt that her new status was an act of grace. He turned and smiled his congratulations to her as she settled into the Mueller pew. Next to her sat both the Mueller boys: Erick, the scholar, and Otto, whom the Great War had badly crippled.

Last of all were the elder Muellers, Hans and Ingrid. Although Peter resented Hans Mueller's being a true Lutheran—not a Scottish Lutheran like the McCaslins. But Hans was a *bona fide* high German Lutheran—his heavy kraut-and-schnitzel bearing made him look more like Martin Luther than anyone else in the church. Or at least the way Peter imagined Martin Luther to look. But Hans was a second-generation German immigrant, so whatever he gained by his being a true Lutheran, he had forfeited by immigrating to America so late. Peter could not be wholly charitable, for it was the Germans, not the Scots, who were responsible for the Great War. Also, the Muellers remained manual laborers, involved in the kind of heavy work that prompted Peter's grandfather to refer to them as the "coal people."

Peter now smiled at the coal people. Hans and Ingrid smiled back. Peter did not know that, even as he smiled, Hans had always thought of Peter and his wife as the "cow people." After the dairyman had finished acknowledging those in the vicinity of the second pew, he and Kathleen shifted their attention toward the front, to await the Reverend Stoltzfus and the little choir that would begin the service.

The McCaslin retinue also included Peter's sister, Isabel, whom everyone referred to as Izzy. She had been called Izzy for so long, she thought of the nickname as a normal one. But *normal* was not a word that came to mind when describing Izzy. She was better at being by herself than with others. An avid reader of the Bible, she jangled her world by quoting its passages often and boisterously. Izzy was the earthly mooring for Peter's ego. However high he allowed his Scottish sense of royalty to soar, Izzy would be there to call him down by reminding him of his being related to someone who didn't fit into the family portrait. For the high social climate Peter had dreamed for himself in King of Prussia would never include a person like Izzy.

Peter watched his sister out of the corner of his eye as she took her seat in the McCaslin pew. The McCaslin nemesis and, unfortunately, half owner of the dairy farm. According to their late father's will, the dairy was to be transferred to both their names and owned on a fifty-fifty basis. The strangest part of the will, though, was that he had stipulated that the cows (almost all Guernseys) be given to Peter and the two new trucks to Izzy. And whenever Peter acted too persnickety toward Izzy, which he tended to do with some frequency, she was quick to respond, "Don't forget, Peter, the trucks are mine."

So was half the dairy. Who could say why old McCaslin gave the trucks to Izzy? Some said it was because he knew Peter needed a daily reminder that Izzy was a McCaslin. Perhaps then Peter would not forget to take care of her or deny his sister her rightful income.

As Peter was about to return his focus toward the altar, his eye caught a glimpse of something sparkling near Isabel's throat. "Izzy, what are you doing with that?" he asked, pointing to the diamond brooch she had pinned where her scarf gathered at the top of her sweater.

"Papa gave it to me . . . it's mine—just like the trucks."

Peter's eyes flashed fire.

His contorted look made Isabel seem relieved they were in church.

"You silly woman! That's not the kind of thing you wear with a cardigan. You get that back in the safe-deposit box at the bank first thing in the morning."

"Maybe I will and maybe I won't," Isabel said. She didn't like the way Peter thought he could boss her around. The brooch belonged to her and Peter had no say about it. But she would hate to lose it. Knowing it was worth hundreds of dollars, she decided it best to go ahead and put it back in their safe-deposit box when the bank opened the next day.

Peter's glaring at her was interrupted as the organ came to life and Reverend Stoltzfus entered the sanctuary. It was time for the doxology. Peter would soon be singing with the entire congregation, and for the moment he put aside his never-ending assessment of those around him. He now directed his thoughts toward God. But sometimes his mind strayed. Once during the service, he wondered if there might be any legal way to get the dairy trucks in his name.

Peter was absent from his surroundings for a while, then remembering he was in church, he stiffened himself like one coming out of a faraway trance and lifted his voice in singing "Praise God from whom all blessings flow." Even as he sang, the thought of those blessings that were Izzy's—the trucks, the brooch—filled his mind again. He contemplated the legal maneuver he could employ to get them away from her, which of course spoiled his hymn.

❧❧❧

Not every doxology is sung in church.

A grim, small pageant of survival was taking place at the same time by a railroad trestle on the far side of the McCaslin farm. Peter McCaslin hated squatters. He wanted no riffraff on his place. But Peter didn't know they were there, and they didn't know he owned the rusty car that had become their home.

2

On Monday Isabel noticed that the Muellers' coal truck was parked between her house and the dairy barn. The sight alone was perhaps of little consequence, except she also saw that the green bronze rooster on the weather vane was crowing to the east.

"The wind's in the east! It's a sign," she sighed.

Then Otto stepped into her view. He had a strong upper torso, the kind made for loading and unloading coal. But the rest of his frame was too slight to suggest he was meant to do such work. Moreover, one of his legs was clearly shriveled, the result of a war injury. Yet in spite of the disability, his eyes remained keen, piercing. Otto's whole demeanor gave one the idea he was a lover of life.

Isabel, on the other hand, had not yet experienced enough of life to make her very sophisticated or worldly-wise. She was built stocky but moved with agility. She might have been considered attractive were it not for her eccentricities. Though she had reached age twenty-six, she still retained many of the characteristics of adolescence. Innocence rarely suspects it exists, however, and so Isabel was quite at home with who she was.

The geometry of what Isabel surveyed seemed all out of whack—the weather vane pointed east and the coal truck, too, which was parked cockeyed also faced eastward. Otto looked as though he was pointed nowhere. To most it would appear that the rooster, the truck, and the man were three separate events that had no relationship to one another. But Izzy was a prophetess with an eye trained to correlate such events. Further, she was better able than most to see the "hand of God" in ordinary things. Isabel listened. The angels sang brief hallelujahs, and then the sign was fixed. Leaving her window of observation, she poured herself a cup of coffee into a brown clay mug, then set about returning to her housework.

"Lord, if you would like me to take a cup of coffee to Otto, let him glance this way," Isabel said out loud. Then for just a moment Otto straightened and looked out across the world, slowly turning toward Isabel's direction. Many would have seen this as the Lord ignoring her trivial prayer, but to Isabel it was a clear sign. So she poured a second cup of coffee and hurried out to the coal shed where Otto was scooping the black chunks into the bin.

"Mr. Mueller, it's a brisk morning," Isabel stated as she offered him the coffee.

"Thank you," Otto said shyly, then reached for the mug.

"Is black all right?"

He nodded.

Otto needed a break, and Isabel looked thrilled to supply it.

But Otto was uneasy. He had always felt it difficult for an ordinary person like himself to make conversation with a prophetess like Isabel. She showed little interest in everyday life. Still, he thought he'd give it a try. He inquired how the dairy had done during the coldest part of the winter. The herd had done fine, she said. Still, his one simple question led Isabel to comment on a myriad of subjects. Considering the nature of the separate things she talked about, her disjointed ideas contained amazingly smooth transitions.

The McCaslin baby, she said, had been born in the time of snow and was therefore "bound to live a pure life." She gave her view as to why the weather was so unseasonably warm, then shifted to expound on why she thought Luther was correct about transubstantiation and the pope.

"Mind you, I'm not against Catholics," she said. "But they'd do better to think over some of their doctrines before they wrote them down. False teachers will abound in the time of Gog and Magog, don't you agree?"

"Yes, ma'am," agreed Otto. "That'll be about the time of the great tribulation, won't it?" Otto wanted very much to talk to Isabel, but he needn't have worked so hard at it, for she could carry on a whole conversation by herself. Finally it occurred to Otto that what Isabel thought was a *reasonable* conversation was quite different than his own view.

Then she smiled and he knew he was doing okay.

"Times are hard, Otto Mueller. Do you think Jesus will come back soon?"

"I don't know, Izzy. I wish He'd return and write a check to cover all my recent losses on Wall Street. Then I could quit delivering coal." Otto's attempt at humor was meant to help relieve Isabel of the load of responsibility she seemed to carry over the end of the world.

She smiled again, but then turned serious. Maybe after thinking about his remark, she didn't see it as very funny—the Lord coming back merely to write him a check. After all, there were kingdoms that had to be "plucked up" as she put it, and "earthquakes that had to fall on divers places."

So she rebuked Otto, quiet as he was, with "The world is a serious place, and if you give the Devil much ground, he'll plant his own crops on it."

"Yes, I can see that," Otto said. But he wasn't altogether sure that he did.

Neither of them spoke for a while, and then Isabel shattered the awkward silence. While nodding toward the weather vane, she said, "The rooster's crowing to the east. When the wind's in the east,

God's up to mighty things. That's Exodus 14:21."

"Well . . . thanks for the coffee, Izzy. Where kindness is greatest, there stands the throne of God," he replied, feeling foolish about reciting a cliché.

"Is that in the Bible?"

"No, but it otta be," he laughed.

Isabel didn't laugh. Anything a person added to the Word of God was a dangerous matter to her. She saw such a thing as flippant and an invitation for false doctrine. Turning abruptly away, Isabel strode back to the house.

Otto admired how she walked so purposefully. Isabel seemed to carry herself as if she had a divine role to play even in a small town like King of Prussia. But then she lived the kind of life that enabled her to bear the heaviest of truths. And it was bad to lay a truth aside. It could be misplaced or stolen or subverted into a false doctrine.

Isabel stood at her kitchen window and watched Otto, who remained out in the yard stock-still, perhaps thinking over her odd prophecy. She had not heard Otto chuckle at her manner as he turned his back on the McCaslin house. He was finishing his coffee now while leaning against the cab of his father's truck. What she could not imagine was that Otto was in fact recalling how Isabel had once distinguished herself among the families west of King of Prussia in September of 1918, some twelve years earlier. Isabel was only fourteen then, yet she had boldly predicted that the armistice would come on the third of November. She got both the month and year right and was just eight days off on the actual date.

During her teens Isabel developed a love for Shakespeare, which she had inherited as a gift from her father. They had both fallen for the bard, probably because his plays sounded much like the King James Bible. Soon Isabel discovered that, with very little effort, the two could be joined in her mind and "trained to see the similarities."

Neither prophecy nor Shakespeare came to Isabel in a slipshod fashion. To her thinking there was always order in the way God went about running the world. And if she could turn her head just right and squint, sometimes she could get a peek at heaven's logic. When asked how she happened to be so close in predicting Armistice Day, she responded that she had learned biblical numerology from an old Shiloh scholar, who had studied with the former New England Second-Coming cult.

Wars ended in an era of peace, or what's known as the Shiloh *eight*, the symbol of perfection. This is especially true when added to the number *three*, the symbol of the infallible Trinity. These of course equal the number *eleven*. Since November is the eleventh month, it was therefore the perfect time for the Great War to come to an end. By similar errant numerology Isabel had also arrived at the third of the month.

But if she was off about the exact date, she was

only "slightly off," which was how most people thought of Isabel McCaslin. But she was the last one to notice her own eccentricities. Isabel remained convinced that things went better when the wind blew to the east—something that rarely happened in Pennsylvania. South was the direction in summer, north in the winter. So when she awoke Monday morning and found the rooster crowing to the east, it was indication enough to believe at least a small miracle would strike somewhere near King of Prussia.

✤

Isabel's brief exchange with Otto—the eldest son of the "coal people"—was not mere happenstance. It had significance, because it was how Otto ended up with the coffee mug. He had meant to bring it back to the house but was more than halfway home when he realized he had forgotten to return it. By the time Otto arrived home, however, he was no longer thinking of the mug but of Exodus 14:21. After a quick shower he looked up the passage. It was a reference to the east wind that divided the Red Sea so the children of Israel could pass through it.

"Papa," Otto said, "has Izzy McCaslin always been so eccentric?"

Hans, who once again was a victim of severe back pain, muttered, "Eccentric? The voman is crazy."

"Maybe, but always?"

"Vell, Otto, let me put it dis vay. Old McCaslin got mixed up with der Shiloh people vhen she vas pretty young, and after that she couldn't talk about anything but Jesus coming again."

"Did she go so far as to set a date for the Second Coming?"

"Nope, not that I know of. But she alvays thought it vas a good idea to keep lookin' east, just so, in case He did come, she'd get the first look at all the fireworks. But she talks about it so much she sets ve good Lutherans on edge."

"Papa, wouldn't she be pretty, if she wasn't—"

"Nutty?"

"Eccentric," insisted Otto, choosing a kinder word.

"Vhat's this?" Hans asked. "You're not getting sveet on der loony, are you, son?"

"No, Papa. But the wind was in the east this morning."

"You all right, Otto? The east . . . so vhat?"

Otto decided to drop the subject.

At eight o'clock the phone rang. Hans answered. "Okay, Izzy. Okay . . . yes . . . I'll tell him." Then he hung up.

"Otto, Izzy says you got her coffee cup. You havin' coffee mitt the loonies now?"

Otto thought it best not to try to describe the situation by which he had inadvertently brought home Isabel's coffee cup.

But Hans wasn't quite through. "She said to tell you that Genesis 44:2 has something to say to you about how a pilfered cup can be a sign, and she said to tell you der rooster vas still crowing to der east. Now, vhat exactly did she mean by that, Otto?"

Otto shrugged.

"C'mon, Otto," Hans insisted.

"It's in Exodus 14:21, Papa. I'm going to my room."

When he had been gone for a moment, Ingrid came in from the kitchen.

"Ingrid, Otto's got Izzy's cup . . . it's in the Bible."

"Are you all right?" Ingrid was as uncertain as to where the conversation was going as Otto had been earlier. "Hans, you think Otto is lonely?"

"Lonely? No. How could he be? He's home again mitt us, Ingrid."

"Yes, but we're old and he keeps to himself a lot. Not at all like Erick."

"He never vas like Erick." Hans shrugged off the seriousness of her words. "He's alvays kept to himself. Still, I don't know about Izzy McCaslin. She voted for Herbert Hoover. Vorse than that, she told everybody. Ve never should've given vomen the right to vote. It's people like Izzy who are responsible for the mess ve're in. I tell you, Ingrid, Herbert Hoover vas put in office by crazy vomen."

Ingrid ignored Hans' outlandish political views. She had heard them all before. "I talked to Mrs. Chadwick the other day," she continued. "She says

28

he hardly ever says anything to her at church. And Mrs. Paul Johns says he never says a thing when he drops off her load of coal. I don't know. I think he's lonely, Hans."

Hans grunted, and the grunt ended his interest in the subject.

Almost an hour went by at the Muellers before Ingrid heard Hans snoring. She turned and saw that he had fallen asleep. The newspaper stood tented over his chest, and the bridge of his spectacles had pressed a little red circle on the side of his ample-sized nose. Ingrid recognized the nightly ritual of Hans' life. He would soon awaken, grunt, and then raise himself laboriously off the couch and lumber toward the bedroom, with his slippers scuffing their worn braided rug.

She picked up the Bible and was about to read a short passage before retiring, when the phone rang. "Who could be calling this late, Hans?" Ingrid muttered as she laid the book back on the lampstand and got up from her chair.

Hans was so sound asleep he didn't hear her question, though he did hear the phone ring a second time. Lifting himself to rest on an elbow, he looked in Ingrid's direction as she picked up the earpiece from its tarnished brass hook.

"Hello, Ingrid Mueller here."

"Ingrid, Otto took my coal scoop!" Mabel Cartwright was abrupt.

There was no need for Mabel to identify herself—

Ingrid knew who it was. Still, her manner was unusually stinging, as if she had spent considerable time building up for her outburst. She spoke at a rapid pace, perhaps so she wouldn't lose her nerve.

"Why, Mabel?" Ingrid asked, trying to cool her rising temper.

"How should I know why? Maybe he wants to sell it in the open market over at Valley Forge. It'd bring a loaf of bread at least, and we all know how Otto's come back to town begging a living from those he slighted back before the war. I hope he's grateful that you and Hans took him back in and gave him a job. It's hard enough for people who *aren't* crippled to get work these days."

Ingrid bit her lip and stood there, silent.

"Ingrid? Ingrid! Are we cut off?" Mabel probed the crackling, electric garble of the country line.

"Mabel, I don't want to talk to you anymore," Ingrid said, her voice trembling now.

"Well, you just tell Otto that I'm on to him and—"

But Ingrid wasn't interested in hearing the rest of what Mabel had to say. She had slammed down the earpiece and broke into tears.

"Vhat's the matter?" Hans asked while struggling up from the couch. He placed a firm hand on his lower back, then straightened his glasses.

"Why won't they give him a chance? Why do they suspect him just because he came home broke? Otto's had enough . . ." Ingrid's voice trailed off and then after a moment, she said, "Mabel called Otto a cripple."

"Busybody!" Hans seethed. "Mabel Cartwright is the devil in a dress! Mean people like her go on forever."

Fresh tears streamed down Ingrid's cheeks. There was no use denying it. She knew that Otto had been the latest subject of gossip around King of Prussia. Ever since Christmas Day when he had shown up to put their world back together, those townspeople with too little to do had made up their minds to attack the Muellers.

"Vhy is she calling so late?" Hans asked.

"She thinks Otto stole her coal scoop."

Hans' features turned a deep red. "You know vhat Vill Rogers said the other day on the radio?" He didn't wait for Ingrid to respond. "He said he never met a soul he didn't like. Just proves he never met Mabel Cartwright. Vhy, she should be horse-vhipped. I'd like to give her a . . ." But whatever Hans would like to give her was suddenly muffled. His athletic gesturing as he was railing Mabel had wrenched his back so that he now writhed in pain. Limping into the bedroom, he collapsed onto the bed exhausted. Ingrid followed him in. "Vhy, Ingrid? Vhy do I have dis bad back and Mabel Cartwright is as healthy as a cow? She's like a cow in a lot of ways."

It was not a kind remark, but both of them grinned. Soon they were laughing out loud. Then

Ingrid lay down beside Hans, and they held each other and laughed some more.

"Vhy vould Otto steal her scoop," laughed Hans, "vhen he might have hit her mitt it?"

Hans was acting a bit hostile, yet the idea caused Ingrid to resume her giggling. "Why not, Hans?" she said. "Hitting Mabel with the back side of a coal scoop wouldn't hurt her much, and maybe it'd teach her to be a little nicer."

"Maybe, but it'll take more than a coal scoop to teach that voman how to be a real human being."

They finally stopped their laughing, and the house grew quiet again. Before long they were ready for bed and had lain back down to sleep, when Ingrid said, "Hans, listen . . . do you hear anything?"

"The vind's blowing a little."

They remained still for a while. The wind was blowing. The house always creaked a little when the wind blew, but there was something more. Or was there?

Ingrid thought she heard something. She thought she heard someone weeping. No. Yes. Maybe. Then nothing. But Ingrid was rarely mistaken about what she thought she heard. "It's what you think you hear that's heard with better ears than those the Lord gives for mere listening," she whispered.

Hans heard neither Ingrid nor what Ingrid thought she heard.

It seemed to Ingrid that the wind was blowing

like a friend who entertains by whispering little things to avoid having to speak of bigger things. The house creaked. The wind blew. And the house creaked yet again.

❧

The same wind had deepened the chill at the railroad trestle, where Ernest Pitovsky wondered how he could drive back the final onslaught of winter. He longed to see his small family completely shielded from the elements. He now viewed himself as an absolute failure for subjecting them to such harshness.

Nevertheless, they looked on him as their sole protector. To his wife and children, Ernest was a big man, big enough that he alone might banish the cold and shelter them from the biting chill of the night.

Regardless of how big he appeared to them, however, Ernest knew his problem was much greater. He felt little indeed as he watched his family clinging together, fusing their tiny clumps of warmth into a circle of survival against the bitter cold.

The wind moaned. Ice formed on the damp grass.

Not far away the McCaslins and Muellers slept on in mansions filled with warmth and hope.

But inside the old car, alone in the darkness, the Pitovskys continued to hold one another and pray for the wind to die down and for the sun to begin its rising.

3

Kathleen McCaslin was nursing her little one when Isabel came in from the dairy barn. Peter sat at the table sipping his coffee. Their baby had been born in December, during the terrible snowstorm that folks in King of Prussia were still talking about. It had snowed off and on ever since, except recently the snowfall had diminished and become less frequent. And each was melting a bit before the next one fell.

Peter set his cup down and scowled at the steaming liquid. "Kathleen, this stuff is the stoutest you've made in a long time."

"Pour some of that good McCaslin milk in it and smile a little, Peter," Kathleen said as she drew her baby in close.

But Peter wasn't the type who smiled for unnecessary reasons.

He turned to Isabel, who was now sitting and immersed in a book. "Izzy, did the help clean the milking parlor gutters and disinfect the floor?" he asked, and then took another sip of coffee, again wincing at the taste.

"Sure did," she answered.

"Did you get Mama's brooch back to the bank?"

"*My* brooch, you mean."

"Well, did you?"

"Sure did."

Izzy gave her simple reply, then settled back into the gray winged chair. She noted the splatters of milk on her faded blouse—splatters gotten in the separating room, setting the blue milk free from its yellow cream.

Peter went on. "Gotta keep the barn floor clean in case it snows again this weekend."

"Snow's over!" Isabel said.

"Oh, the snow's over, is it? Middle of February and the snow's over. And just who told you that?"

"I figured it out when the wind changed. It never snows after the wind changes to the east. It didn't in '27 and it didn't in '29, and it won't this year either."

"Is that so! The east wind's just gonna hold back all that gray weather, is it?"

"Well, it held back the Red Sea. A little Pennsylvania snow is nothing compared to that."

Peter stopped talking. He scowled once again, not at the strong coffee but at Izzy. He'd rather down a pot of lousy coffee than try to have a sensible exchange of words with his sister. Izzy wasn't quite normal, so it was nearly impossible to carry on a normal conversation with her. But Peter's attempt at ending their talk didn't stop Isabel. She was eager to go on.

"A couple of miracles already blew in," she said. "I got a new coal scoop."

Peter laughed, but when she glared at him, he quit his laughing and decided to pursue her line of reasoning. "So I guess the Lord just dropped the scoop into the east wind and then blew it right into the coal bin."

"No. That nice new coal man left it for me."

"Could it be, Izzy, that he just plain forgot it?"

"Nope, it was a miracle."

Peter shook his head and once again tried to end the weird conversation.

"You know what the other miracle was?" she then asked.

Peter drained his cup. "No, what?"

"This!" Isabel held out an antique pewter picture frame. But the picture that was once in it was now missing.

"Where'd Benny's picture go?" he asked.

Isabel smiled. "It's just gone. Benny's gone now!" She bit her lip, then picked up her Bible and started reading. She always read slowly, tracing the text with her right index finger while her lips silently spoke the words.

Peter set down the coffee mug and shook his head.

A few hours later Isabel had gone to her room,

and Peter and Kathleen sat down together on the edge of their bed.

"Okay, Kate, where's Benny?"

Kathleen shrugged. "I don't know."

Benny had haunted the McCaslin family for almost five years. In the summer of '26, when Isabel was twenty-two, Benny had come through town selling Bibles. Isabel withdrew some money out of the Clabber Girl Baking Powder can—her stash for the hard times she had predicted were coming—and then purchased a Bible from Benny. Their meeting sparked an odd romance.

While Benny was "working the area," he drove out to the dairy every night to see Isabel. Often she would make him dinner, then they'd talk. Who knew all they talked about? But in the middle of August, Benny suddenly up and left. Or as Isabel put it at the time, he "disappeared like the flock of nativity angels in the Gospel of Luke." She took his leaving pretty hard. From then on, her life became a kind of long, deep sigh.

Apparently Benny had given her a sepia photograph of himself, which later became a sacred icon to her. She removed twenty more nickels out of the Clabber Girl can to buy the pewter frame that would hold his picture. Isabel stared at the frame the first thing in the morning when she got up and again at night before going to sleep. She had convinced herself that he'd return one day, although she admitted he had never made any such promise.

Isabel tried to pretend Benny's leaving didn't bother her. Yet Peter and Kathleen saw that, after Benny had left, Isabel grew increasingly remote from her family and friends. The distance put between herself and the world was a gap she filled with the Bible. In Isabel's case, this preoccupation seemed to steal her mind at times. She developed a curious and unbreakable tendency to preach to people. It wasn't long before others began seeing her as deeply troubled. Soon Isabel was working in the dairy by day and keeping mostly to her room at all other times. Peter felt it was a lot to blame on Benny, but there was no denying that most of Isabel's strange behavior could be traced back to her broken heart.

On the current evening everyone went to bed early.

Peter and Kathleen were drifting off to sleep, when Kathleen jostled Peter back to semiawareness. "I'm glad he's gone, Peter."

"Who's gone?" asked Peter groggily.

"Benny, the Bible guy."

"Yeah, the wind's in the east. Benny's gone. Maybe it's a miracle. Maybe Izzy will get better now."

"I don't think I'd say she's cured yet. What did she say about a coal scoop?"

"She said the coal man gave it to her," Peter replied. "She said it was a sign."

Kathleen groaned.

Out on the roof of the dairy barn the weather

vane rattled in the wind, and the old bronze rooster stared toward the horizon where the sun would come up after the cold night had passed.

And as far as Isabel was concerned, when the rooster looked east, everything was looking up.

4

Mary Withers watched as the Mueller truck pulled into her driveway. "Mama! It's Uncle Otto!" Alexis shouted.

"Yes, *Uncle* Otto!" Mary replied. She had allowed Alexis to call Otto her "uncle" only because the Muellers had insisted on it. While Mary was still uncomfortable with this new intimacy, Alexis held no such compunction.

It was funny that Alexis wouldn't have thought of calling Erick Mueller her uncle. Already in her mind Alexis knew what Erick knew: There would be a wedding. Then Otto would for sure be her uncle, Erick would be her papa, and old Hans would be her grandpa. It was all heady stuff for Alexis.

How can they all be so certain there will be a wedding? Mary wondered. How could the entire town have become so settled about which Mary herself was still so unsure of?

Otto had exited the truck and was now knocking at the door. Mary quickly opened it, smiling.

"How much coal, Mary?" he asked.

"The weather's been warmer, so I don't need much . . . a quarter of a ton?" She smiled again.

Otto grinned back. He looked an awful lot like Erick, that is, without the mustache and the wire glasses.

"Do I get a cup of tea after I get it unloaded?"

Mary nodded. "I'll see what I can do."

"Hooray!" Alexis cried.

Unloading the coal took much longer when Otto delivered it as compared to his brother, Erick. Otto's bum leg had slowed all of life down for him.

After the coal was finally in the bin, he knocked at the door once again. This time Alexis let him in. Otto doffed his black gloves, and soon the three of them were seated at Mary's round oak table. Alexis had pushed her chair back from the table a bit, so now she could hold her cat, Caspian, on her lap.

"Here, Otto," Mary said as she handed him three dollars for the coal.

"Nope! Hans said it's free from now on. Can't charge family." Otto grinned once more, then he folded Mary's fingers back over the bills and pushed her hand gently toward her side.

But Mary pulled away. Not to be outdone, she reached up and stuck the money into the flapped pocket of Otto's coal-smudged shirt. "Otto, Alexis hasn't had one of her asthma spells since Christmas, and I'd much rather buy coal than ephedrine. So you tell your father I appreciate his kindness, but I want to buy my own coal." Then the phone rang.

"Hello ... yes, hello, Mabel ... yes, Otto is here ... you want to talk to him...? Oh, you don't." After a long pause, it became clear Mary was feeling the pain of something Mabel was saying. Finally Mary said, "Yes ... I'll tell him ... I'm sure Otto didn't mean to ... Now, Mabel, simmer down. There's got to be another explanation ... yes, well, all right then ... I'll tell him. Good-bye, Mabel."

Mary hung up the earpiece. "Humph!"

"You know, Mabel has the same effect on my mother," Otto said. "What are you upset about, Mary?"

"Otto, Mabel's accusing you of stealing her coal scoop."

"Now, why would she think that?" Then he remembered, and his face lit up as if a light went on in his brain. "I went from her house directly over to the McCaslins. I'll bet I left it over there. I'll see if I can find it and clear my name," he laughed.

Mary wished to change the subject. She glanced at the teakettle and then at Otto's cup. "How's the tea?" she asked.

Otto nodded "fine," then smiled. "Mary," he said shyly, "Erick's got a case for you. Mama says he's bitten down on this relationship harder than she's ever known him to bite. And I'm glad. It's my turn to be an only child—even if I am thirty-two years old. At least I will be as soon as Erick's out from underfoot."

She looked at him and forced a smile back.

"The two of you sure do look good together, especially sitting in church. The whole town's buzzing! One of these weekends, when Erick comes home from Syracuse, he's for sure gonna bring a ring."

Mary was only half smiling now and appeared a little shaky.

"Oh, Uncle Otto, are we gonna be engaged?" Alexis was all excitement.

Mary seemed uncomfortable at first; then she burst into laughter. "Yes, *we* very well could be engaged soon, Alexis."

Otto laughed so hard that he dribbled tea on his sleeve.

"We come as a package, Otto. I'm afraid if the Muellers get one of us, they'll just have to take us both."

For the moment Mary tried to concentrate on enjoying Alexis's excitement. Yet she couldn't help but wonder if the events of the Christmas before had pushed her and Erick faster toward marriage than they might otherwise have gone. And she still carried a measure of guilt over letting go of her late husband. Further, Mary wasn't altogether convinced that Erick understood what he was getting into. Even if he was willing to take on being responsible for a sick child—though she despised thinking of Alexis that way—she wasn't sure that he had accepted the possibility of Alexis's asthma continuing on for years to come.

But Mary knew herself to be a worrywart. It was very clear that Alexis and Otto had no trouble with the idea. She did feel the joy of belonging to the Mueller family. Sitting with Hans and Ingrid in church gave her a feeling of contentment, stability. The frenzied, lonely years of struggling through the trials of widowhood were now passing. The way Hans and Alexis got along, and the way Erick seemed taken by her little girl was more than wonderful to Mary.

Mary had been so deep in thought, she didn't notice Otto and Alexis staring at her. Both had the same calm and serious look that she probably displayed when she was lost in her thoughts. It was the entire gravity of everyone that set Mary to laughing to a degree she rarely allowed herself. All three of them were soon howling like her. It was a wonderful moment that fell like a warm rain on their arid togetherness.

"This is what I like about being a part of the Mueller family," Mary said, and then she touched Otto's arm. But feeling guilty, she immediately drew back. "Otto, was there ever anyone for you?" As soon as the words left her mouth, Mary wished she hadn't asked. It was too personal of a question, and she suddenly felt she was being impertinent. "I mean . . . I'm sorry, that's really none of my business. Please forgive me."

Otto talked as freely with Mary as he had ever talked with anyone, but he was stingy with his comments. He was not overly stingy, however. He just preferred to listen to others talk about themselves than to spend the time talking about his own affairs.

"Oh, Mary ... please, it's all right. Yes, I thought I was in love once. Recently. In fact, just last summer. Before the stock market crashed." Otto suddenly realized he had gotten into the habit of marking the events of his life in relation to Black Tuesday, as it had come to be called. "But I came to my senses and never got around to popping the question. I'm *crippled*. It's not a hard word for me to say, but a very hard word it seems for others to live with. Anyway ... let's face it, Mary, nobody should have to live with—"

"Stop it, Otto!" Mary's words cut short whatever self-deprecating excuse Otto might have given.

But Otto sensed that she was more troubled about it all than he was. "Anyway, she died." Then he ceased recounting his story as if his next words were difficult to articulate. "And now, Mary, there's not much of a future for a thirty-two-year-old bachelor who drags a leg. I did have a cup of coffee with Izzy McCaslin, though. Papa says she's crazy, but Izzy's house and your house are the only places other than home where I've ever been offered a cup of anything. 'Course with Izzy, coffee and prophecy come together."

"By the way, how's the McCaslin baby?" Mary asked, hoping to move the conversation far away from Isabel.

"Fine. Izzy says a baby born in a December snowstorm's bound to be a good child, 'pure as winter and a blessing all her life.' They say Izzy likes to quote the Bible, but I've noticed that if she can't think of a Scripture she needs, she just makes up and inserts one of her own right there on the spot, right beside the good words of Moses and the apostles."

"How did the McCaslin herd stand up against the winter this year? Are all the cows still producing? I don't know what we'd do for milk around here without their dairy farm." Once again Mary tried to steer their talk away from Izzy.

"Izzy says the cows are fat and full of cream. She says the McCaslin cows are fatter than the kine of Bashan. She says that's from the Book of Amos, but it could be from the Book of Izzy—I don't know," Otto laughed.

Mary gave up her attempt at changing the subject. It was quite clear that Otto wanted to talk about Izzy. So she let Otto continue on, interjecting once in a while to encourage him, "What else did Izzy say?"

"She said that the wind was in the east, just like in Exodus when God performed the miracle at the Red Sea. She didn't say, though, what the miracle would be. Only that there would be one, and that

miracles are the grin of God that often come to people who don't often catch God grinning." Otto paused, then blurted, "Mary, did Izzy really predict the armistice in '18?"

"I've heard she did. But she's predicted a lot of things, and some of them would have to come about sooner or later."

"Yeah, it's like all those monkeys."

"What monkeys?" Mary asked, perplexed as to where he was going with this.

"They say that if you placed an infinite number of monkeys in front of an infinite number of type-writers, one of them would produce a Shakespear-ean play. So I suppose if a person like Izzy makes enough predictions, one of them is bound to come true."

They both chuckled at the comparison of typing monkeys and Izzy's prophesying.

"Know what I think, Otto? I think that old man McCaslin got her thinking those wild thoughts when she was just a little girl. And it's been said she changed after that Bible salesman, Benny, left King of Prussia without a word and hasn't been heard from since. Izzy had fallen for him, you know. I've often wondered if that had never happened, if she wouldn't have been pretty . . ." Mary's sentence dragged to a series of pauses and then stopped. She could see that Otto was troubled.

"Pretty what, Mary? Pretty normal? Is that what you were going to say?"

Mary's silence spoke loudly that it was precisely what she was about to say.

Otto stood. He then slowly smiled. "Mary, I can't say if Isabel McCaslin is normal or not. I do know that there's a consensus among those of King of Prussia that she's not. But life is hard, and sometimes those who ought to reach with understanding reach only with criticism. Some people's minds get sick. Other people's legs don't work right, and it's not always because of any fault of their own."

"I'm sorry, Otto," Mary said. She reached out and touched his arm again. "I've always been too critical. It's my worst fault. Can you please forgive me?"

"It's nothing, forget it," he said. "But Mabel Cartwright told my parents last night that I returned home a dependent cripple. It's strange that I don't mind saying those words myself, but whenever someone else uses them, then I'm offended. Izzy gave me a cup of coffee. That's all I know. She's eccentric and I'm crippled, and we recently shared a moment of life together in the middle of a community that will probably never think much of either of us."

"Otto, the wise one! That's who you are," Mary responded. "Maybe Izzy's right about the miracle. Maybe you're it. Old Hans still speaks of your homecoming as the only miracle of life that matters."

The conversation turned uncomfortably deep, so Otto smiled and said, "Mary, speaking of old Hans,

he's going to be mad that you paid for your coal. You know, giving you coal is how Papa shows you he loves you. And he's pretty particular when it comes to his coal revenue, especially now when times are hard. He doesn't even give coal to the orphanage."

A kind of miracle happened, whether Izzy had anything to do with it or not. Otto had opened up more that afternoon than he had in a long time. "Blab, blab, blab," he said as he turned to leave. "Mary, I'm sorry I've run on so. You've been very patient."

But Otto hadn't talked all that much; it just seemed like it to him.

They walked to the door; then Otto put back on his gloves and cap and turned to Mary. "Erick's home this weekend. I'll see you in church. I can't believe how religious I'm becoming." Otto laughed as he shuffled to the truck.

Mary wasn't laughing, for she couldn't believe how insensitive she had been to Otto. Further, she felt as though a disturbing congeniality was casting a shadow over her deepening relationship with Erick.

She continued thinking about this till Alexis suddenly interrupted her reverie. "Mama! Did you see a tear on Uncle Otto's cheek?"

She had, but she couldn't remember when exactly. Was it before or after they had discussed Isa-

bel. . . ? It was before, but what was there to shed a tear over?

"Mama, Mrs. Johnson says that some people cry because they can't help it, because they have *repression*."

Mary restrained herself from laughing, then said, "Not *repression*, Alexis, but *depression*."

"Does Uncle Otto have it?"

"No, honey. I don't think so." But Mary wasn't sure.

Otto had come through some dark days of loneliness and financial hardship. Who can say when tears become cumulative? Perhaps crying is what the eyes do when the mind can't make sense of things.

"Mama, has Uncle Otto got a girlfriend?"

"No, honey, he just had coffee with a woman."

"With Izzy McCaslin?"

"Yes, with Izzy."

"Ebby Johnson says that Izzy knows when Jesus is coming again, and Izzy won't tell the Lutherans because they all think she's odd."

"Nobody knows when Jesus is coming back, Alexis."

"But Ebby Johnson says that Izzy knows, and that she also guessed the very day that the war ended. Is that true, Mama?"

"Well, I don't know. Maybe she just got lucky, honey."

"If Uncle Otto keeps having coffee with Izzy,

maybe she'll tell him when Jesus is coming, and then he can tell all of us Lutherans. It would be a nice thing to know."

Mary laughed, but not Alexis.

Otto was mesmerized by the sunshine. He knew it was still two hours before the afternoon milking, so he decided to return Isabel's coffee cup. The cup itself wasn't a very good excuse to drive all the way out to the dairy, except that now he had a second motive—to see if he'd left Mabel's scoop in the McCaslin coal bin. Having no more coal to deliver, these two small excuses provided him a legitimate reason to visit Isabel. He hoped Hans wouldn't mind if he used the coal truck for something as personal as returning a coffee mug and clearing his name with Mabel Cartwright.

The truth was that Isabel fascinated him. She didn't appear crazy to Otto, a bit compulsive maybe. Her chatty life-style seemed to serve as a sort of verbal bandage for some deep inner wound. There was one other thing he'd noticed: He felt that when he was with her, he could talk more freely than just about anywhere. Isabel carried a disability that made her wonderfully human, that had endeared her to him.

How had a woman so in love with all that was good become the brunt of such derisive gossip? he wondered.

When Otto arrived at the dairy, Isabel was standing on the front porch. She waved a wide hello, flailing the air with her upraised hand. He waved back from the open window of the truck, then parked and hopped out onto the gravel driveway. He only had time to take a few steps when Isabel met him by the side of the truck.

"I brought your coffee cup back," Otto said.

" 'He who steals my cup becomes my slave,' " she laughed. "Genesis 44:10. 'Thus did Benjamin become the slave of Joseph.' "

"Is there anything in the Bible that speaks of a penalty for stealing coal scoops?"

Isabel became quiet. "You mean it wasn't a gift?"

"No, Izzy. The scoop belongs to Mabel Cartwright. I have to take it back right away."

"Owe nothing to perversity... for slander is its swift reward. A hard woman will execute a debtor quicker than she will countenance a gift."

"That's not in the Bible, is it?" Otto asked.

"No, not really... but it otta be!"

Isabel then hurried off to the house and soon returned with Mabel's coal scoop.

"There!" she said, handing it over to him. " 'From him that would borrow, turn not away.' "

"Saint Matthew?"

"That's right! Matthew 5:42," Isabel said.

Otto waved the scoop a little and said, "Neither

a borrower nor a lender be."

"The Bible?" she asked.

"Nope, that's from *Hamlet*."

"Do justly, love mercy."

"And what does that mean?"

"It means you should read the Bible more," Isabel said. "It should be a lamp to your feet and a light to your path. It's a two-edged sword dividing to the piercing asunder of the body and the spirit and the joints and the marrow, and a discerner of the thoughts and the intents of the heart. The Bible is God's Book, a bestseller year after year, that will never return unto Him void, but will accomplish that which He pleases and will prosper in the thing whereto He sent it. It is twice blessed. It blesses him who gives and him who receives—"

"Wait a minute, Izzy. That last line was from *The Merchant of Venice*. It's not in the Bible."

"Oh ... well, I sometimes forget where I read what."

"You want your cup back or not?" Otto asked.

"How about if I fill it back up and we have a cup of coffee together?"

Otto was hoping she'd say this.

Isabel raced back into the house and filled both his cup and one for herself, then rejoined him out on the porch. "Let's sit on the swing, want to?"

He did, yet he approached the swing cautiously. Sitting there with her would bring them close together.

She handed him the mug of coffee, saying, " 'Lord, let this cup pass from me.' "

"Izzy, that's a poor way to use that Scripture. Our Lord wasn't having coffee when He first said those words. It could be considered sacrilegious." But Otto knew it wasn't at all sacrilegious when Izzy said it.

Isabel didn't stay with the subject, though. "So how did you hurt your leg, Otto?"

He wished she wasn't so bold in her approach but would slow down some and remember at least a few of the rules of propriety. "Well, I was injured in the war."

"You're lucky only one of them was hurt. A clumsy nurse dropped Jonathan's little Mephibosheth when he was a baby, so that he was lame in both feet for as long as he lived. That's in Second Samuel 4:5."

"I know a verse of the Bible too."

"So do I," she quickly responded. "I know a lot of verses. 'His Word have I hid in my heart that I might not sin against God.' "

"Wanna hear my verse?" Otto asked.

"I will listen all day for the hearing of the words of His law."

That didn't sound like a true verse to him. "How about this one?" he said. " 'Let every man be swift to hear and slow to speak,' which seems to say that it may not be good to talk all the time, even if you are quoting from the Bible."

Otto could tell the idea was new to her.

She wasn't offended but sat silent for a while, turning the words of the verse over and over again in her mind.

Finally Otto interrupted the unusual quiet that had enveloped them. "Feel the pleasantness of silence, Izzy." It seemed hard for her to grasp what he was saying; therefore, he added, " 'Offer unto the Almighty the gift of solitude. Bind your words lest they break the thrall of quiet, for in quiet it is easier to find God than in the abundance of words.' "

Isabel's face revealed she was transfixed by Otto's words, by the new idea that silence was a virtue. She was so enraptured she didn't notice that her cup had tilted and spilled coffee on the porch floor. Otto had also ceased talking, and so in an absolute quietness, the two of them learned that a silent togetherness can transcend words.

While Isabel sat there, Otto did an audacious thing. He stuck a folded piece of paper in her shirt pocket, then rose quietly from the swing and walked away. He had participated in a kind of miracle, but she didn't see it till he was gone.

He had helped her to be still, to discover quietness again. She watched him walk away, and then another miracle occurred. She saw the world that surrounded his awkward retreat. He was limping. He always limped, but yet he was whole. As Isabel sat there feeling the sun on her skin, she sensed she was seeing life for the first time.

But it was hard for Isabel to deal with this truth,

that God lived not in her constant talking. That He sometimes fared better in the silence, in the blues and the greens and the ochers of the world. Then she felt the wonder of togetherness that's born when airy silence takes the place of leaden conversation. This reality swept over her so powerfully she didn't hear the rumble of the coal truck's engine as Otto headed back to town.

After some long minutes she released her hold on silence. Or rather, it released its hold on her. She thought about the miracle of the east wind again, wondering if a new kind of person wasn't being born within her.

What had just happened? She was sitting on the swing having coffee with a crippled man, when he pointed out for her the beauty of silence and how it can be more refreshing than the endless speaking and reciting that usually occupied her poor mind.

Her gaze dropped to the floor, and she caught sight of the small pool of spilled coffee that had almost dried now. She also noticed the piece of paper Otto had put in her pocket. Lifting it out, Isabel unfolded the paper and began reading.

*Come, God, rip the tongues from all my bragging
  chatter.*
Kiss my endless stream of words with silence.
*Let me see your towering solitude above the shabby
  noise of living.*
I would see it all, and yet hear nothing.
As the east wind blows without a sound—

As the silent grass sings only with its waving—
As the trees come wordlessly to fruit and find their
anthem in the mute prism of the rainbow.
Life comes as a voiceless orchestra
never heard by those who talk their way
through all God's soundless symphonies of grace.
   Otto Mueller, March 15, 1929

Of course, it's highly unlikely that a single experience would transform a lifetime of compulsive behavior. But some compulsions are open to instruction. Isabel McCaslin was given a gift that day—a gift she'd spend the rest of her days unwrapping—from a man familiar with suffering. Her boundless flow of proverbs had been stopped behind the levee of a new truth: Solitude was the better way to live, and silence had much to teach her.

The Reading Railroad tracks first appeared on the McCaslin farm in 1897, crossing over a trestled gully at the back of their 160 acres. Now in 1930, on the third week of February, the old tracks made a good walking path for Isabel. She believed the warmer weather would push spring to mid-March and so set out on her yearly trek around the farm a little earlier than usual. She meant to walk the entire fence line to make sure the fences were still intact following the hard winter months.

Isabel passed the gully where the trestle had been built. Alongside rested a dozen or so abandoned automobiles. She would have hardly given the junk cars a second look, if it wasn't for her catching a glimpse of something pink moving through the weeds, which quickly disappeared inside one of the cars.

One of the results of the difficult times was the horde of vagrants who wandered coast to coast on the railroads looking for work. Such folks often subsisted on spilled grain from the railcars or whatever else they could get as they drifted into various towns and begged door to door. And any junkyard that happened to be located near the railroads soon became a good place to build a fire out of the wind and hole up till the worst of winter had passed. But the flash of pink that had caught Isabel's eye seemed too small and fleeting to have been one of these hoboes.

Without hesitating, Isabel rushed to see who or what it was she had seen escape into the deserted automobile. She half slid her way down the railroad embankment, then threaded herself through the damp matted grass. Isabel then slowed her pace as she approached the car where she'd seen the pink figure disappear. Pulling open the door, she peered inside. There were no seats, but crouched down against the back was a thin woman who looked extremely ill nourished. And clinging to her were two small children. Though it could be said they were trespassing on McCaslin property, Isabel felt that she was invading their privacy.

"Excuse me, ma'am, but . . . uh . . . I'm so sorry to intrude. . . ." Isabel struggled to stop her stammering.

The woman crawled to one of the passenger doors and, grabbing hold of the rusted roof, maneuvered herself into a standing position outside the car.

In the morning sunlight Isabel could tell the

woman was even thinner than she first had thought. Her dress was also thin—much too thin to keep her warm outside the car. Springtime was getting near, the air becoming milder. Still, it was far from being warm enough to prevent the fragile-looking woman or her little ones from freezing.

"It's too cold to be living in this old car, ma'am," Isabel said. "It's a wonder you're not all sick."

The woman coughed and then cleared her throat. "My husband's been out trying to find a job. He said he'd stop by the Salvation Army and pick up some blankets before coming back. It's the nights that get to us mostly. I don't feel too safe when he's away—there's a lot of riffraff walking these tracks."

It didn't seem to occur to the woman that some might consider her to be "riffraff."

"Have you been eating regularly?" Isabel asked.

The woman didn't answer, but she didn't need to.

"When did your husband leave?"

"Two days ago."

The children, who at first remained hidden behind the woman's tattered dress, had grown braver and were now taking peeks at Isabel.

Isabel was shocked at the children's scrawny appearance. Their biggest feature seemed to be their eyes.

"Ma'am, you can't stay out here!"

Isabel meant no harm; still the woman began

crying. "Please let us stay till my husband comes back. Maybe he's found work. Maybe that's why he isn't here yet. But whether he did or not, he may be bringing us some blankets." She then covered her mouth with both hands and wept, her narrow shoulders heaving with each sob.

"Now, now," Isabel said, "you just quit that!"

Her rebuke was so gentle, the woman stanched her tears and looked at Isabel.

"Ma'am, I want you to come with me. We got an old shed where we used to let a hired hand stay. It's got a bed and stove and there's a cistern in the separating room. God doesn't want you to keep your little ones out here in this junkyard. Will you come?"

An uncertain look came over her, but soon she smiled weakly.

"Yes," the woman said, "but I'd better leave a note for my husband."

Isabel agreed, and the woman pulled out a stub of a pencil from the torn pocket of her dress. But as she dropped to her knees to crawl back into the car, she reversed her action and stood again. The woman then looked past Isabel's stare to the figure behind her. "Ernest!" she shouted.

Isabel swung around to face a gaunt man, who was approaching her cautiously. The toes of his shoes were but a scuffed-up gathering of shredded leather, so wet from the spring thaw that Isabel wondered how he'd survived with almost nothing between himself and the ground.

"Ernest," repeated the thin woman. "Oh, Ernest, you got some blankets!"

The blankets looked rather worn, but to people who had been living on the bleak edge of life, they were considered good fortune.

"Who is this?" Ernest asked as he gestured toward Isabel.

"I don't know. I only know she's offered me and the children a real roof and a coal fire."

"Not just them but you too, mister. My name's Isabel McCaslin. I own this land . . . well, me and my brother do. We own it all except for the railroad right-of-way."

"My name's Ernest Pitovsky. This is my wife, Helena."

"Well, hello to the both of you. And who might these two be?" Isabel asked, smiling at the children.

"The girl is Katrinka. She's five years old. The boy is Freiderich and he's three."

Isabel was struck by how her saying the children's names had conferred upon them an instant dignity. They both smiled in unison, displaying their tiny, beautifully white teeth.

Helena turned to Ernest and asked, "Did you find any work?"

"No, just blankets. They're the best I can do for today. But maybe I'll get work tomorrow or when spring comes."

Isabel suddenly knew what she must do. She

wouldn't just offer them the old shed with its bed and roof. No, she thought of something much better—the gift of dignity. She would offer the man a job. For when a man had dignity, the state of his shoes and mackinaw didn't much matter. But she wouldn't hurry the issue.

Isabel thought about Otto. She'd thought of him quite a bit the last few days and about putting to practice his doctrine of silence. Listen first, talk later. Then when there was enough silence, she'd bring up the job offer.

So she decided to try to do more than just rescue the Pitovskys from their living in a junkyard. Yet rescue and dignity were one and the same—both were the business of God. Isabel was well aware that she herself had been rescued. Now she had found the Pitovskys. This must have been what kept the rooster crowing to the east. Life was about to change for these four weary children of God. God had come to the McCaslin farm, perhaps to show them how big His family truly was. Peter might not see it this way, but it was clear enough to Isabel. Her eyes lit up as she contemplated her mission.

"Ernest, you and your family can't stay here in this car any longer. This is my property and I say you can't stay here. Now, I just promised your wife and children our little shed. 'Course it won't be free. I'll have to charge you something."

"Yes . . . well, we would expect to pay, ma'am," he replied.

His "yes" was like music to Isabel's ears.

Then Helena said, "But we haven't any—"

"Money?" Isabel interrupted. "Well, you will when Ernest brings home his first paycheck—Ernest's money." She paused. "That's funny, don't you think ... *Ernest money?*" Isabel laughed, but her new friends did not.

"Like I just told Helena, I don't have a job," Ernest said.

Things then got quiet. It was time to talk, time to offer the man work. But slowly.

"Oh, are you looking for work?" asked Isabel, as if his whole demeanor wasn't screaming the fact. But she took her time. Dignity was not something to be given too hastily. She had to offer it and then stand back, so they could pick it up and put it on at their own pace. It had to be their choice.

"Yes, but there's not a job to be had in all of Philadelphia. That's why we moved out here in the first place. Out here at least there is clean air to breathe, away from the filthy city streets and crowds of people with nothing to do. Every day I ask around town, trying to find anything at all, any kind of work."

"Well, you didn't ask at the McCaslin dairy farm. We've been looking all over for a hired man."

"Begging pardon, ma'am, but I did ask at your place. Is Peter McCaslin part of your family?"

"Yes," Isabel said.

"Because I asked him, and he said you didn't need any help."

Isabel was suddenly ashamed of Peter. She hesitated for a moment, then said, "Peter doesn't really know. He's never been very up on things. *I* run this dairy and I've been looking everywhere for a new hired hand. Are you interested in a job?"

"Well, yes, but..."

"Good, then. When can you start?" Isabel was rushing things a bit now, but this was her first employment interview and she felt great about it.

"Just about any time," Ernest said.

"Good news!" Isabel blurted. "You can start today!"

So the ragtag Pitovsky family gathered up his battered suitcase and a couple of dirty pillow slips filled with the bric-a-brac of their survival and then followed Isabel toward the huge farm—the centerpiece of the McCaslin empire.

They walked silently for a long way before Isabel asked, "Can you milk a cow, Ernest?"

"No, ma'am," he said.

"That's definitely a handicap at a dairy," Isabel said. "Let me see your hands."

Ernest was carrying the bulging pillow slips and also little Freiderich. So he dropped the slips, stood Freiderich on the ground, and showed Isabel his hands.

"Now grab my index finger and squeeze," Isabel ordered.

He did.

"Good grip," she said. "All our cows have four of these kind of things between their back legs."

It was such an elementary lesson that Ernest grinned.

"This is serious, Mr. Pitovsky."

They then walked in silence for a while, when finally Isabel asked, "Are you a Lutheran, Mr. Pitovsky?"

"No, ma'am. I'm a Baptist."

"Pity," she said, "but the Lord loves nearly everybody."

The Pitovskys kept on walking without comment.

"Mr. Pitovsky, are you aware that Jesus is coming again? There could be a time of tribulation on the way."

"Yes, ma'am ... tribulation."

"That's right, Mr. Pitovsky. It's tribulation. Sorry it's been so hard. But things will get better, you'll see. The end is not yet."

"Yes, ma'am."

"You think Jesus will come today, Mr. Pitovsky?"

"I think not."

" 'At such an hour as ye think not, the Son of Man will come.' We live by hope, Mr. Pitovsky."

"Yes, ma'am," Ernest agreed, "but my papa used to say hope ain't nothing more than catching a glimpse of the God of good people."

Isabel puzzled over his proverb, remaining quiet

for a moment. Then she told him, "Well, the Second Coming probably won't be right away. And till it does happen, you're my new employee, Mr. Pitovsky, and your family's guaranteed a warm place to stay. Nothing like a coal fire and jars full of last summer's fruit to tide you over till things get better."

Isabel turned quiet again; then she felt it. The lovely day and the silent concord of God. She was also feeling good about herself. She wasn't quoting Scripture now, but just walking silently with her new friends, doing something good. Otto was right. She didn't have to talk all the time to feel the nearness of God. In fact, there's nothing like giving the beat-up souls of this world a little quiet time in which to recover their dignity. It seemed Ernest Pitovsky was standing a little straighter than when she first met him.

❧

Mabel Cartwright found her coal scoop back at her door the following morning. There was an envelope taped to the bell of the scoop that contained a letter. She lifted the scoop and removed the letter.

Dear Mrs. Cartwright:
I left your scoop by mistake out at the McCaslin farm. I know this must have inconvenienced you. I do apologize and offer you this gift.

Sincerely,
Otto Mueller

The gift was a lengthy poem on how widows often bear the brunt of hard times, on how the world rarely understands those whose busy lives have bypassed their grief. And although Mabel had lived most of her life in a state of loneliness, she now felt her seventy years in King of Prussia hadn't gone completely unnoticed. The final lines of Otto's poem read,

> *Let your aloneness serve.*
> *Let it be a tower that lets you see the world from*
> *high above it.*
> *Then free yourself of all resentment*
> *For those who have more friends.*
> *For solitude is God's glory*
> *weight by which the world is rescued.*

They were strange words that most in King of Prussia would never have applied to Mabel. But after reading the entire poem, Mabel somehow thought better of herself. She stared at the letter a long time, wondering about its meaning. It was a miracle that someone had seen her as she wished to be seen. How long had she been waiting for a real friend? Now her limping coal man had helped her to see the best of truths: Dignity is that bright reflection in the mirror of someone else's warm esteem.

The world is big, but to offer it any aid at all, one has to stick to the small places—helping one soul at a time.

"Oh, Otto!" Ingrid cried. "There's much more to your silent years than we could've ever guessed."

The letter that was on top of his poetry had been addressed to a hospital in New York, in Manhattan. Otto must have placed the child there with the last of his money, before he lost everything on Black Tuesday.

Ingrid struggled to put all the papers back on the nightstand in the somewhat scattered fashion she had found them. But after a considerable amount of shuffling, she felt she had pulled it off with success.

Ingrid then stepped outside and felt the air. It was chilly enough for her velvet-strapped bonnet and gloves, and so she slid them on and left the house, locking the door behind her. In minutes she arrived at the front desk of the Mueller Coal Company. Walking past the desk, she went directly into Hans' office.

Hans was sitting with his right leg propped up on a low stool to take the pressure off his back.

"Hans," she said as she untied the velvet straps of her black bonnet, "Otto has a child."

"Vhat!"

"A child."

"A vife too?"

"No, just a child."

"But how did our Otto get a child?"

"I think he found her in New York after her mother died."

"Vhere's the child now, Ingrid?"

"In a New York orphanage, or hospital. I don't know. I think . . . Hans, I feel awful. I snooped through Otto's papers. I know I shouldn't have snooped . . . I should've minded my own business."

"Now, Ingrid, stop dat. Of course you should've snooped. How you gonna find out dese things if you don't snoop. Snoop, voman, and find out some more. Find out vhere this girl is."

After Ingrid had composed herself so that she was only sniffling, Hans asked, "Does the child have a name?"

"Her name's Marguerite," she managed to say, then broke into crying.

Hans wanted to get up and console Ingrid, but his back dictated that he best stay put. Hasty movements were out of the question.

After a few moments Ingrid had regained her self-control.

"Hans, how can we tell him we know?"

"Simple. Tell him you snooped."

"I can't do that!"

"Then tell him *I* snooped."

"No."

"Tell him the letter blew off his writing desk, and you accidentally read it."

"Accidentally? For two hours I read."

"Some accidents take a long time, Ingrid."

"I can't tell him I snooped. And I won't tell him any lies."

"Vould you rather be a snoop or a liar? It's a hard choice, but you gotta pick one of dem."

Hans was good at solving problems, although Ingrid rarely liked his solutions. "No, I'll just wait and pick my moment. Then when things are right, I'll tell him." She tied her bonnet back on and was about to leave Hans' office, when she turned back and said, "Hans, Otto's a poet!"

"Poet? No, Otto's a coal man."

"A poet, Hans!"

"You can make money writing poetry?"

"Maybe not!"

"Vell, maybe Otto better stay a coal man! Coal makes money."

Ingrid walked straight home, her thoughts boiling over. She thought of how Erick and Otto had been lost to the family. How they were now home again and giving the Mueller name a new significance. Yet, why couldn't they have stayed home in the first place, gotten married and had babies in the normal way? But they hadn't.

And how was she to talk to Otto about things she wasn't supposed to know? Who could she talk to? There was always the minister, but was there no one else?

❧

"Mama, Mrs. Mueller's walking up our driveway," yelled Alexis.

"Mrs. Mueller? Honey, you must be mistaken," Mary said.

"No, Mama! It's really her."

Mary flew to the front of the house while attempting to collect herself. She reached for the doorknob just as Ingrid knocked, yet hesitated a moment to dispel her frenzy. Then after the second knock, she adjusted her hair again and with deliberate aplomb opened the door.

The two women greeted each other. They'd met many times before, but this time it was in Mary's house.

Mary took her things and welcomed Ingrid into her living room. She despised her plain, poorly furnished home, but Ingrid appeared not to notice.

"Can I get you some tea?" Mary asked. She immediately regretted not waiting longer before offering anything so as not to appear too anxious.

Ingrid kindly shook her head, then said, "Mary, am I intruding?"

"Of course not. That wouldn't be possible. You're always welcome here, Ingrid."

Ingrid paused. Mary could see that Ingrid felt awkward and that whatever had prompted her visit was of a serious nature.

"Is this about Erick and me?" Mary inquired, hoping to get Ingrid started.

"No, Mary, dear . . . it's about Otto."

"Otto?"

"Yes, I've learned that Otto . . . has a child."

"A child?"

Mary felt her short interjections were perhaps making it harder for Ingrid to speak, so she determined to remain quiet while Ingrid related everything she'd told Hans earlier.

Ingrid ended by saying, "Now I don't know how to invade his life . . . for the sheer purpose of offering him help, you understand?"

"Yes, I see what you mean," Mary said.

"Otto's so introspective, I'm not surprised he writes poetry. I was in awe at its beauty and am so proud of him. But how shall I tell him, Mary?"

"I'm not sure, but maybe Erick can help."

"Of course! Mary, that's a splendid idea! Erick and Otto have always been pretty close, both before Otto left for the war and then since he returned. Erick must be the answer, or at least some part of it."

Ingrid then had to leave. Mary watched her from the doorway as she walked down the driveway.

Mary felt as if she had been visited by a queen, a queen whose royalty was robed with a heavy compassion for her limping prince. Otto's burden that he'd been carrying all alone now burdened her.

As for Ingrid, she took Mary's counsel to heart and prayed for the weekend to come.

That night Ingrid heard Otto crying. It was unbearable. She wished he'd open up to her and ask her help. But his world remained sealed, holding at bay Ingrid's reaching soul.

8

Ernest was as eager to begin his new job as his employer was to show him the ropes. So Isabel set out to train her new apprentice in how to approach the underside of a Guernsey cow and then coax vigorous streams of milk from each of the teats.

"You don't close your hand all at once like that," she said. "You close the fingers at the top, then slide downward in a rippling motion."

Ernest did it, but not very well. The cow flinched and raised her right hind hoof in protest.

Isabel smiled. "A cow knows a strange hand, but don't get discouraged. Just relax and try it again."

Ernest did, and this time the cow did more than just raise her foot—she kicked at him. Ernest jumped back.

"Let me see something," Isabel said, grabbing his hand. "Oh my! Just look at those fingernails. You'd kick too if somebody squeezed your soft underside with a claw like that." She stepped over to a small wooden box and took out a nail clipper and handed it to him. "Here, trim your nails and then we'll try again."

Before long, Ernest was slowly drawing out the shining white liquid without upsetting the giving cow. Isabel reassured him that things were going to be all right, though she couldn't imagine anyone having trouble getting milk out of such willing donors.

She pulled up another stool and proceeded to milk the next one down the line. A moment later Isabel glanced over at Ernest, who was about doubled over as he applied his new skill. And like the half dozen other employees who squatted beside the docile cud-chewing matrons, Ernest worked hard.

Then Peter entered the barn. Isabel was working on her sixth cow and Ernest his second. Peter took the last bite of an apple, tossed the core in one of the stanchions, and was about to get a bucket and help when he noticed Ernest. He walked up to him, intrigued by his sluggish technique. Peter soon realized Ernest wasn't just a farmhand working like a novice, but someone he'd never seen before.

Peter cleared his throat as he looked down at Ernest. "Excuse me. You new here?"

Ernest nodded.

"Well, I'm Peter McCaslin. And I'm the owner of this dairy. Are you a friend of one of our regular milkers?"

"No, sir. I'm new . . . I just got this job, just today. I was hired by—"

"You were hired by who?" Peter asked. "Like I said, I own this dairy. I do the hiring and I don't remember hiring you." Suddenly Peter recognized the man. He couldn't recall his name but did remember turning him away when he came looking for a job some days before.

Seeing that Ernest was in trouble, Isabel rushed over to try to mediate the problem. As she ran, her milk pail sloshed white froth over its brim. "Peter, the reason you don't remember hiring him is because you didn't hire him. I did."

"Izzy, I own this dairy and I do the hiring!"

"No, you own *half* the dairy and you do *most* of the hiring . . . well, nearly all of it till this afternoon. But today I hired my first employee, Ernest Pitovsky. Peter, this is Ernest. Ernest, this is my brother, Peter."

Ernest, who had stayed quiet during the heated exchange, timidly reached out his hand to shake Peter's.

But Peter's hands remained on his hips. He then glared at Isabel, turned on his heel, and strode out of the barn.

"I don't think he liked me very well," Ernest said. "I suppose I'll be gone by morning."

"Nonsense! He's crazy about you. He always acts a little mean when he finds that I've made decisions without clearing it with him first. But the dairy *is* half mine and you're hired!"

"Yes, ma'am," he said, smiling weakly. "Thank you . . . I really need this job."

Isabel was beaming. "And you have it."

It turned out that Ernest was much better at cleaning the barn than he was at milking. Therefore, once he was finished with the milking, he let the cows out of their stanchions and picked up a shovel. He threw the manure quite a ways to land on top of the near-frozen heap that lay outside the barn's back door.

"Well, Ernest, you're quite a pilot!" Isabel declared.

"A pilot?" he asked.

"Yes, you're a pilot. Somebody always has to *pile it*. We have to pile some of it here, some of it there."

Ernest laughed heartily. Isabel was glad to see him laughing, for she was afraid the brutality of life had stolen every hint of happiness from the new boarders she'd moved into the dairyman's shed.

" 'A merry heart doeth good like a medicine,' " Isabel said.

It was the first Scripture she had quoted in a while. It wasn't a lofty passage, but a verse suited for barn cleaning. *If you could be merry while shoveling manure, you could be merry just about anyplace*, she thought.

Isabel accompanied Ernest back to the shed, where his family was enjoying a warm coal fire. She followed him in and saw right away that, for a family who had been sleeping in a ditched automobile, a new era of peace had begun. Isabel also noticed for the first time that the woman was in fact very pretty.

Helena was busy with dinner, standing over a pan of boiling potatoes. It seemed to Isabel that she'd stumbled upon something holy, a family being held together by the bonds of love and humility.

"Do you believe in the marriage supper of the Lamb?" Isabel asked. "It's in the Book of Revelation."

Ernest nodded, yet he remained unsure of what she was actually asking. "Miss Isabel, you're a godsend to me and my family," he said with a trembling voice.

Isabel was afraid that if she didn't quickly say something he might start crying. "I'm sorry, but the children will have to sleep on the floor tonight," she said. "But by tomorrow night I should be able to round up a couple of spare cots."

"Thanks," Ernest said as he wiped at his eyes. "Helena, supper smells real good. God has looked down on us today!"

"Supper *does* smell good," agreed Isabel, all the while knowing that boiling potatoes didn't produce much of an aroma. "Helena, I admire the way you've kept your family together during such a hard time."

Isabel wished she had stayed quiet. Ernest cupped his hands against his face, and Isabel waited till his silent tears were through rocking his body. It took some time. He had cried quietly, while she rebuked herself for adding to his emotional state by complimenting his wife.

But since she was into it anyway, Isabel decided to offer something from Proverbs. " 'Who can find a virtuous woman? For her price is far above rubies.' Isn't that what you'd say, Ernest?"

Ernest gave his wife an assuring smile and stated that it was what he would've said had he thought it up to say.

Helena, who had left her cooking to comfort her husband earlier, still hadn't said anything. She now resumed her preparations for dinner. Freiderich and Katrinka sat close to the fire, gazing calmly at its warm wonder. The children's faces revealed their being somewhat overwhelmed by the new, pleasant surroundings.

"Ernest, I'm afraid you'll have to work both the early morning and evening shifts. 'Go to the ant, thou sluggard, and be wise. The early bird doth get the worm.'" Isabel was back to her old custom of mixing her own words with Scripture whenever they seemed to fit. "So I'll see you in the barn at five o'clock tomorrow morning."

"That's just fine," Ernest said, not having the slightest notion where the biblical proverbs ended and Isabel's began.

As Isabel was about to leave, Helena began her coughing. Its noisy violence actually frightened Isabel. Ernest pulled from his pocket a badly stained handkerchief and handed it to her. Helena then coughed into the kerchief fresh stains consisting of bright red blood, so copiously that Isabel was afraid she might suffocate from the hemorrhaging. After several agonizing minutes, the coughing finally diminished.

"It's consumption," Ernest explained. "She's had it a long time. It was bad before, but since we lost our house and had to live outside, I'm afraid it's gotten steadily worse."

"Well, maybe now that you're staying in this warm place, she'll begin to get better."

But the Pitovsky family appeared unaffected by Isabel's instant prognosis.

"So far nothing has helped. Life's been like a mountain lately, and I'm not sure we have the strength anymore to keep climbing," Ernest confessed. He folded the handkerchief over the wet stains, then wiped a bit of blood off Helena's bottom lip.

"No need to climb. Faith would be my prescription, faith like a mustard seed. . . . 'Course some of God's greatest miracles—He expects us to help with."

Ernest and Helena looked at each other and nodded weakly.

"Five o'clock, then?" Isabel asked, to confirm the agreement.

"Yes, ma'am. See you at five o'clock . . . before the sun comes up."

Isabel left the family to their modest supper. She thought she'd better get out before Ernest's emotion became contagious. She hurried back to the house and, as she crossed the farmyard, readied herself for the fury that awaited her.

The moment she stepped inside the door, Peter greeted her, shouting, "Just who do you think you are?"

"I'm Isabel McCaslin, half owner of this dairy, by the will of our late father."

"He may have left you half of the farm, but the right to manage it is mine alone."

"Is that so, Peter! Where was that written in Papa's will?"

"It wasn't in the will, but I managed everything for Papa while he was alive, and he meant for me to keep managing it after he was gone."

"Even if that's true, which I doubt, Papa never said I couldn't have a say in who works here. You've hired the help year after year, and I've never once objected. Well, today I hired my first employee, Ernest, and he works here and belongs here just as much as any you ever hired."

"Times are hard, Izzy. We've got to cut every corner we can."

"Then let's cut out the Machen twins—their father has a job and a house. Ernest Pitovsky has nothing. Besides, his wife is sick!"

"How do you know that?"

"Because I moved his whole family into the dairyman's shack."

"You did what?"

"I moved 'em into the old shack. Nobody's using it anyway, and they were sleeping in a junk car out by the railroad trestle. With all the hoboes walking the tracks, it wasn't a safe place for the children. They were all freezing and hungry, so I gave Ernest a job and moved 'em into the shed."

"Children? How many have they got?"

"Two. Freiderich and Katrinka."

"Well, you can just walk over there in the morning and tell him he's fired!"

"I will not, and if you do, so help me, Peter, I'll ... I'll ..." Isabel was shaking now. She couldn't think of what she'd do, so she said, "You'll be very sorry if you interfere." She'd never had such an argument with Peter, but she was determined not to let him do anything to hurt the Pitovsky family.

She stormed out of the room and for the next few days slipped in and out of the house and barn in such a way as to avoid seeing her brother.

On Thursday night a knock at her bedroom door startled her. Feeling anxious, Isabel threw open her door ready to confront Peter if necessary. But it was Kathleen, who was standing in the doorway with a dumbfounded look on her face.

She held out a letter. "Here," Kathleen said, "this

came for you today. Izzy, Peter's right, you know. That family's got to go."

Isabel seethed inside. She snapped up the envelope in Kathleen's hand, then slammed the door. Plopping down on her bed, Isabel studied the envelope. She recognized the script and then tore it open with a flourish.

Dear Isabel,
The church-folk are abuzz with your deed,
Mostly condemnation, I'm afraid.
But I for one, know how it feels to live
And sleep on hopeless sidewalks.
So, thank you for keeping a pocket full of life
And using it like taffy in a famine.
Dearest Isabel, I find myself increasingly in love
with
All the things you are.
Am I too forward?
Forgive the gush and honor the best
And holiest part of my affirmation.
Compassion is a garment worn by those
Who gift wrap dignity for those who've
Forgotten their
self-worth.
And dignity! What is it, after all, if not
The right God gives us to find our
Purpose in the world?

Isabel looked up from the letter. It was achingly beautiful. She noted that the last half included one of Otto's poems. Yet, because the entire letter was written so poetically, it was hard for her to tell the difference between the place where the letter ended and the poetry began.

> Dignity is born in heaven,
> give it and you behave like God.
> Find within yourself what makes virtue holy
> But hold it not within yourself.
> For if you do, the holiness of all you found
> will be cankered by your pettiness.
> Turn your back on those who will not sacrifice
> their own worth
> To provide worth for someone else.
> Teach shame to value light,
> so that it may stand upright,
> Not in arrogance
> But in the honest knowledge that it has worth.
> When you have lived best for God,
> Others who despised themselves,
> Will see their worth,
> Feel your rescue and lay the joy of their redemption
> At your feet.
> Above all where hope is wounded
> Suture its torn flesh with compassion.
> And where the scar was,
> Will be stitched the name of grace.
> Otto Mueller, March 19, 1930

The balmy weather was clearly to Hans' displeasure, for he liked it cold. Then people ordered coal. But now the orders had dwindled, and the Mueller business began to fall apart. There was a strike the previous fall in Appalachia that had led Hans to buy up a large reserve of coal. This was to increase his profit later, after the impending frigid winter had escalated the prices. But the weather and numbers hadn't worked out as he'd planned, and so Hans was stuck with a mountain of coal lying in his storage yard. Otto saw that business was bad and wished the weather had cooperated more to Hans' liking. But it seemed that since Hans' back was keeping him down for so many weeks, perhaps the good Lord was allowing him some time to rest up for a colder, more lucrative winter the following year.

Soon after arriving home late Friday night, Erick learned of the task Ingrid had awaiting him regarding his brother and the "talk" they needed to have.

Erick agreed to help Otto with the Saturday morning coal run and, at the same time, try to speak with him about what Ingrid had discovered.

The next day the two brothers had finished all the deliveries and would've returned home early, except that Erick suggested they stop and have lunch together at the King of Prussia Café. They walked in, and before long Helga Bruening, a short woman with an accent thicker than Hans', had taken their order—soup, bread, and coffee. Following the crash of '29, the scarcity of employment combined with the rising cost of meat had out of necessity turned people into vegetarians.

Helga trudged past their table on her way to the kitchen. She smiled, as she always did, through clenched teeth. Her failure to open her mouth when she grinned seemed rooted in the idea that a full, open smile might cause her to appear excessively happy. And such happiness must be avoided so as not to contribute to frivolity or unwarranted cheeriness.

When their soup and bread arrived they both glanced up toward heaven before picking up their spoons in recognition of the family custom of saying grace. But since Hans and Ingrid weren't there to force the issue, a simple look in God's direction seemed to suffice.

Erick then set his mind on how to get Otto talking about the things Ingrid—his snoop of a mother—had recently found out. "Do you like Eliot?" he asked.

"Eliot who?"

"You know, the writer—T. S. Eliot."

"Oh, that Eliot," Otto said as he let out a laugh.

His lighthearted laughter made Erick's soup taste better.

"Yeah, sure. Only I'm surprised you know about him. He never taught math at Syracuse University, did he? But why the question?"

Erick played it safe, being careful not to be discovered. He planned to sort of smoke Otto out into the open without his knowing what was going on. " 'We are the hollow men—' "

"That's 'We are the *stuffed* men.' "

"Oh. 'Headpiece filled with straw, leaning together—' "

"Okay, Erick, so why the sudden interest in Eliot?"

Erick abandoned his subtle attempt now, jumping to where originally he'd hoped to wind up. "Otto, Mama saw the letter and poems on your nightstand. And as far as she can tell, you have a protégée or a child you're supporting?"

Otto nodded and then seemed to retreat behind some dark façade.

Erick now questioned whether he'd be able to get through. "We're all very concerned about you, brother. All those years you were out of touch had to be hard on you. It must've been much more inconvenient than you hoped it would be." Erick knew he was going about his light interrogation the wrong way.

But Otto didn't clam up.

"Inconvenient, Erick?" Otto started out tentatively, then gradually picked up speed. "Life's seldom *convenient* and almost never easy. These past months following the crash of the stock market have been the hardest I've ever known. Frankly, I hit bottom. For a while I wanted to just lie there and die. Then I came home. But even that wasn't easy. I felt ashamed, like I had come crawling back . . . exactly like Mabel Cartwright told Mama on the telephone. I tried to get work in New York, but nobody hires cripples. Not even the warehouses or drayage companies had any jobs. I moved slow and knew my bum leg wouldn't let me be a stevedore. So I came home with sixty dollars, convinced that when it was gone, I'd just die."

Erick knew the rest but let Otto run on all the same. He listened with a pain in his gut over all that Otto had suffered.

"I'm not the fastest coal scooper in eastern Pennsylvania, but I love Papa more than he'll ever know for letting me help out and actually paying me for it. Scooping coal and paying my own way again somehow gave me a hope I thought I'd never find again."

Sensing that Otto's confession was coming hard for him, Erick sought to turn the conversation.

"Mama says your poetry is good, maybe even great!"

"She's too good a mother to be a good critic. But she's right about one thing. I have a daughter ... well, kind of a daughter. There was a little girl and her mother who lived across the hall from me back when I had my own posh apartment and the stock market was providing me a good living. I had a relationship with the mother, Renee LeBlanc, a divorcée. Renee was very sick with cancer, which claimed her life faster than I've ever seen anyone die. But she suffered more from the anxiety over leaving her child with no one to look after her than from the disease itself.

"I was in love with Renee. At first I thought my love for her was more out of pity, but it wasn't long before I knew her cancer had nothing to do with it. I loved her little girl, Marguerite, as well. Renee saw that I loved her child, and that alone hastened our romance toward a commitment to each other. It felt like we were in a desperate race to get married before the disease stopped everything.

"Then she was gone, taking all reason and sense with her. She passed away one month before the big crash on Wall Street. I know if she had lived, we would've married. But it was not to be.

"Marguerite became my only passion. I had never seen a small child deal with death. She didn't cry much. I kept her at my apartment as much as I could. She just stared straight ahead and held on to me for dear life. She wouldn't let go, and when I'd try to pry her loose, she'd look at me as if I was an ogre with no feelings. That's often how I felt.

"After the funeral, Marguerite stayed mostly at the orphanage that was next to the hospital where Renee died. In fact, the hospital and orphanage were both part of the same organization. The problem was that Renee's huge medical bills were attached to Marguerite's expenses at the orphanage later on. Renee had signed over all her assets to the hospital to protect her daughter after she was gone.

"I wasn't prepared to deal with the terror Marguerite felt without her mother. The people at the orphanage weren't mean to her, but they were all strangers. Marguerite cried most of the first month. Then she sort of disappeared into some hideaway corner of her soul where she didn't respond to anyone, even to those who were kind to her. She shut out everyone but me, Erick. She needed me so much that I just had to go see her every day. I loved her, played with her, and took her presents.

"Before Black Tuesday I could easily pay for her care at the orphanage. But after the crash I was ruined. I told the orphanage director I'd keep paying as best I could. Before I knew it, though, I was evicted from my apartment. Then I struggled for a few weeks with life in the streets, using the rest of my money to stay in half-dollar flophouses till coming back here last December. I've been sending my income from delivering coal to the orphanage, but it's not enough to cover all the weeks when I got behind. I don't know how much longer they'll tolerate Marguerite as a charity case."

Erick had been sitting there quietly listening, but now Otto seemed out of words.

"Don't be angry, Otto, but Mama read your letter to the orphanage."

If Erick thought his brother would erupt in anger, he was mistaken. Otto went on calmly, "I could never be angry with Mama or with any of you. But I honestly don't know what to do."

"Well, for starters you might include us in your circle of confidence. Trust us. Who knows what all of us Muellers could do if we put our minds to it? We can help. We *want* to help. Let us in your life, Otto."

It was more straightforward than Erick wanted to be. He knew Otto wasn't being selfish but only serving his introverted nature. Otto could be hard to pry out of his shell, and he'd grown to love the silence inside himself. Erick was thinking of a gentler way to soften what he'd just said when Otto broke in.

"You've already done so much," Otto said. "I wish I knew what to do. What would be best for Marguerite? I'm not sure the orphanage will release her, except to the state, without some guarantee of payment. And where can I get that kind of money? I doubt if Mama and Papa have that much, not that I'd ever ask them. But even if they could afford it, it's not their problem."

"Will you just allow us to help you think through all this?"

"If you think it's best."

"I do, and so do Mama and Papa."

"Then what's next?"

"Next is family. Family's where all things heavy find a common strength for the bearing." The statement was somehow too poetic for Erick; it was the kind of thing Otto might have said. "Times are hard, Otto. Things may look bleak now, but they're not impossible." Erick felt better about this last statement.

Otto agreed silently. Silently in his mind was how Otto did his best negotiating.

He seemed to Erick to be as real as a person could be, but he stored words in his tightly guarded mind, like gold coins, and spent them conservatively to buy only the most necessary of utterances.

They got up and paid their bill, while Helga clanked around their table picking up dishes.

By the time Erick and Otto reached home, Ingrid was taking a German potato casserole out of the oven. She'd baked it specifically for their lunch, so neither of them had the courage to tell her they'd just eaten large bowls of soup less than an hour before at the King of Prussia Café. One didn't tell Ingrid such things. And so they sat down to eat yet again. Hans was summoned in to say the prayer. This made Otto and Erick feel their overeating was more acceptable to God, who, knowing all things, was sure to understand why they didn't tell Ingrid they'd already had lunch.

All conversation was sacred among the Muellers, although there was nothing too sacred to report. Thus Erick asked Otto if he'd read aloud one of his poems. At first Otto waved his hand in refusal, for during all his years at home he had never read his verses for them. After all, it had just been discovered he even wrote poetry. It was no use wasting his breath saying he could read them one if they liked. Instead, Otto answered by going to his room and returning with a handful of pages.

"Hey, don't read us all of 'em—just one," Erick protested.

"Do you want poetry or not?" laughed Otto.

Soon the whole family was laughing. It was a pleasant respite from the heaviness all around them. Then Hans and Erick and Ingrid listened intently as Otto read from the pages. Hans seemed to struggle to understand. Erick smiled a lot. Ingrid relished every syllable.

"Vhat does it mean?" Hans asked. Perhaps because he'd spent most of his life reading coal-order forms, Hans puzzled over why a friendly person would arrange words in such a way as to baffle another person.

"Oh, Hans, you don't ask what poetry *means*," Ingrid said. "You ask what it *feels*. Poetry isn't to get facts but to apprehend beauty."

"Vell, I don't apprehend it! I'm sorry." Hans stuck

out his chin, and while he remained physically at the table, mentally he left the circle of highbrows that his plain old coal-delivery truck was financing.

"Otto, read some more!" Erick pleaded.

"No, some other time," Otto said. "Papa shouldn't feel left out in his own home. He's the keeper of our feast and has a right to hear things he understands and enjoys."

"Oh, your papa is an old German who could use a little culture," Ingrid shot back.

"Vhat I need is cold veather. You can't sell coal vhen March thinks it's July. By the vay, how vere the deliveries, boys?" Hans grumbled as he asked the question.

"Slow," said Erick. "Hardly enough to keep Otto busy."

"Maybe now I'll have more time to write poetry, Papa!" Otto said, smiling.

"You'd do better to write up some coal orders, son, and leave der poetry to people who can afford it." Hans paused, then grew reflective. "Von boy a professor, von a poet. Vhat's a hardvorking man supposed to do vhen der country needs coal, and his sons have more brains than necessary?"

It was Hans' honest assessment, and Erick and Otto just stared at each other, neither of them knowing what to say.

Then Hans abruptly changed the subject. "Otto, tell us about dis little girl you feel such an obligation to. Vhat's her name?"

"Marguerite." Otto blurted the name before he had time to collect his thoughts. His reconciling with his father the Christmas before hadn't totally eliminated the fear he had felt toward him when a teenager.

"Oh, Hans, you make a bull in a china shop seem like a feather bed!" Ingrid thumped him on the chest.

Otto cleared his throat. "It's all right, Mama. It's a fair question. It's time I open *all* the luggage I brought home with me."

Otto told them everything he had shared with Erick earlier that day at the café. They all listened, and Hans' face softened.

"Mabel Cartwright vill have a good time mitt dis."

Things got quiet for a moment, then Erick slapped his brother on the shoulder and said, "Otto, times are tough and money's short! I don't know what you can do or want to do with Marguerite, but you make the decision, and we'll stand by you all the way. We know you'll do the right thing."

Hans was slower to speak. "Your mama's right. I'm a pigheaded German! The coal business isn't so good now, but ve'll vork on dis mitt you till you're satisfied you've done all you can for Marguerite."

"I've been thinking," Ingrid said, "maybe we should get a lawyer and see what can be done about fostering the little girl."

Otto's eyes lit up at the idea. Hans just grunted.

"Here, Ingrid? But ve're old and my back hurts!"

"You'll get better. Besides, it isn't your back that's stiff. It's your compassion. It's those vertebrae just back of your heart that could stand a little flexibility," Ingrid said with a resolute tone. "Boys, take care that you never marry a hardheaded, hardhearted German with inflexible vertebrae."

"Dere's nothing wrong mitt my wertebrae. Vhat's wrong is that my family thinks I deal in gold not coal." Hans knew he was being cranky. He turned toward Otto. "Son, listen to your mama. She knows about dese things." Then Hans attempted to stand up by bracing his stocky arms on the table's edge and pushing slowly downward. All his weight on the table caused it to creak and tilt in his direction and the leftover potato casserole to slide his way.

He finally got to his feet, tottering and holding his back with his right hand. As he began to hobble away from the table, he said, "Ingrid, vhen you talk to der lawyer, ask him for a discount and remind him der coal business hasn't been too good."

Otto jumped up from his chair, ran over to his father, and threw his arms around him. "Papa, thank you!"

"I didn't exactly say I'd do anything, Otto. I only said ve'd talk to a lawyer."

But Otto hugged him all the tighter.

Hans raised his thick hand and patted Otto on the shoulder.

It couldn't be said whether or not Hans returned Otto's hug. But if his back had felt better, and if hugging had come easier to him, he probably would've held his son for a very long time.

Dr. Drummond was surprised to see the

dairy truck pull up in front of his house at nine P.M. He watched Isabel as she slammed the truck's door and walked toward his front porch. As she was reaching with her finger to push the doorbell, Drummond suddenly appeared in the doorway, insisting that she come in.

"Dr. Drummond, I've hired a new man at the dairy, and his wife has consumption." Isabel wasn't good at chitchat when there was a crisis at hand. "I was wondering if you'd have a look at her."

"Now?"

"Well, yes! *Now*'s when she's bleeding from the lungs! Tomorrow she could be worse off than today. So she needs your help now!"

The physician smiled. Although her approach was rather blunt and abrasive, he couldn't deny that her logic was right, irrefutable in fact. Immediately was usually when sick people needed to see a doctor. So he yelled a good-bye to his wife and grabbed his black bag and hat. Before leaving, though, he hurried to the back of his dispensary and picked up some sulfa and a cheap celluloid inhaler. Then he returned to the front of the house and accompanied Isabel out. To avoid having to be driven back home, Dr. Drummond decided to take his sedan and follow her and the truck back to the McCaslin Dairy.

While pulling open the door to his car, he turned and shouted to Isabel, "Hey, why didn't you just call me?"

"Because Peter and Kathleen don't approve of my helping the Pitovskys. I thought it best not to use the phone and get them all riled up. You know, 'Blessed are the peacemakers.'" Right away Isabel wished she hadn't quoted the Scripture, feeling as though she were somehow betraying Otto.

Drummond groaned at her reply. The only time he hated practicing medicine was when it landed him in the middle of a family quarrel. But there was the Hippocratic oath to think of, so he got in his car, started it, and made a quick U-turn while flipping on the headlights. Before he knew it he had fallen behind the dairy truck by a good three blocks. It wasn't that he had to keep up with Isabel to avoid losing his way—he'd been out to the farm many times—but he wanted to arrive there at the same time Isabel did to avoid an uncomfortable situation that might arise with Peter and Kathleen.

Fortunately, when he got there Dr. Drummond saw nothing of Isabel's brother and sister-in-law. Isabel led him down an unlit path that ran past the barn to the dairyman's shed. Once inside, they could feel the glow of the coal fire that had warmed the tiny interior. The two children were lying on cots in the corner so sound asleep that the happenings of the moment were nonexistent.

"Dr. Drummond, this is Ernest Pitovsky."

Ernest reached out his hand, and the doctor shook it. They nodded a cordial greeting to each other, saying "glad to meet you" without the necessity of words.

"And this is his wife, Helena," Isabel said.

There were fresh splatters of blood on the sheets. In a weak attempt, Helena tried to adjust them and cover the stains before collapsing back onto the bed. "Doctor, I'm sorry you had to come. I don't feel all that bad, but Izzy insisted."

"I'm quite happy to come. That's what doctors do. Please, don't apologize."

Dr. Drummond then took the stethoscope from his bag and began his examination. A high-pitched rattle but no fever. Isabel was right—it was consumption. But Helena was wrong. Her illness was serious and mustn't be allowed to progress any further or it could mean death.

He left the sulfa powder along with the inhaler. He knew they might give Helena some relief but that such relief would only be temporary. After quietly closing his bag, the doctor said good-night, then stepped outside the small shack, followed by Ernest and Isabel.

When he was certain that Helena couldn't hear them, Dr. Drummond said to Ernest, "Mr. Pitovsky, your wife is very ill. I recommend that Helena be moved to Reser Sanatorium in south Philadelphia for complete bed rest and hourly treatment. If this isn't done, she might not live much longer."

Ernest felt as if he'd been kicked in the stomach. "Doctor, will this treatment be expensive?"

"I'm afraid so. Though Reser is one of the least expensive sanatoriums, it could still run as much as seventy-five dollars a week."

Ernest just stared at the ground, rubbing the back of his neck with his hand.

The doctor continued. "If you're a United States citizen, then the state might help you—up to ten dollars or so a week. But you'd need to come up with the rest of it."

They all knew the sum was out of the question. Isabel was paying Ernest well, but twenty a week wasn't nearly enough to do it.

"For how long?" asked Ernest.

"Four to six months maybe. It all depends on how she responds."

Their little gathering then turned toward chit-chat, but the conversation was strained because the two men didn't know each other, and anyway, Ernest wasn't one for small talk.

Dr. Drummond had excused himself and was

backing out of the driveway, when Isabel turned to Ernest and found she was at a loss for words. She couldn't think of anything to say to encourage her new employee. What was she to do now? The amount of money the doctor mentioned presented a real challenge that would take a lot of thinking to pull off. The economic hardship brought on by the stock market crash had resulted in an every-man-for-himself philosophy. Such a situation had led even "good people" to turn their backs on one another, to avoid taking on more responsibility than they could handle.

Isabel and Ernest returned to the shack to check on Helena. Isabel studied them in the heavy silence that encompassed the room. The Pitovsky family looked to be the models for Vincent van Gogh's "The Potato Eaters," which was mostly what they ate. Finding herself preoccupied in trying to figure out how to help the Pitovskys, Isabel wondered if her actions would make the townspeople as mad as Lucifer, "when his tail drug a third of the stars, and he came down to the earth furious in his descent." Again she thought of Otto and chided herself for using Scripture in a way that complicated things.

Isabel wasn't sure how to say good-night to Ernest and Helena after hearing such dismal news. She decided to pray out loud. Loud was exactly how she did it and without asking their permission. She simply clamped her eyes shut and launched into it. And so as if trying to compensate for the fact that heaven was a great distance from the dairyman's shed, Isabel raised her voice to make it easier for God to hear: "Lord, things only seem impossible because we can't figure out how to get them done. Help us think better and then have the courage to do what we've thought up. Amen. Milking's at five A.M.," she said, barely separating her prayer from her work orders.

It was now close to eleven o'clock—much later than a dairyman ought to stay up—but Peter was waiting for her when she walked in the house.

"Izzy, I told you, those people have to go!" he said, unconcerned about softening his opening words with diplomacy.

"Those people are the Pitovskys! You can't say their names, can you, Peter? For the moment you do, they won't be *those people* anymore. They'll be real people with real names just like the McCaslins. As long as you don't name them, they'll only be things, and things are discarded easier than people."

Peter grabbed her and placed his hand on her chin, then forcibly turned her face until their eyes met. "Izzy, those people—"

"The Pitovskys," she insisted.

"Are going! Do you understand?"

But she didn't understand. "Mrs. Pitovsky's sick. Dr. Drummond says she needs to go to a sanatorium. Otherwise she'll die."

"Dr. Drummond? You didn't involve him in this, did you?"

"Of course! He's a doctor, so I asked him to come out and take a look at her. She's got consumption and needs treatment—now!"

"But this woman's not our responsibility. Can't you see that?"

"Peter, do you believe in God?"

"What's that got to do with it?"

"God loves Helena Pitovsky just like He loves you and me, and I believe God wants us to help others when we can. She's coughing up blood and possibly even dying. We've got to do all we can to save her. Please help me, Peter. Mrs. Pitovsky needs a little hope."

"Well, we can't afford the kind of hope she needs! It would cost money—money we can't spare right now."

"But hope is more than just money. Hope is catching a glimpse of the God of good people!" *Where have I heard that before?* Isabel wondered.

"Izzy, you're out of your mind. You always have been. And people all over this town know it. You know what they call you? 'Dizzy Izzy.' You go around talking to God and quoting the Bible and poking your nose in things that are none of your business. It's been embarrassing watching you make a laughingstock of the McCaslin name. But this time you've gone too far!"

Isabel bit her lip. She knew Peter was right about her reputation, that people saw her as some kind of crank. She often felt alone even in her own home.

But Peter wasn't just expressing how the community felt about her—it was primarily how he felt. Her own brother seemed the most ashamed of her, that she was a part of his life. His remarks made her burn inside. She bit her lip again, then turned to face him.

"Peter, I know what people say and I'm sorry for the embarrassment I've caused you and Kathleen. Sometimes God gives us something to be done and it isn't easy and nobody understands it. Still, it must be done anyway."

"No, it must not be done! This is our home too and it's our dairy, so it'll NOT be done!"

Peter's shouting woke up the baby, who was now crying in the next room. "See what you've done, Dizzy Izzy!" He then stomped away to the bedroom to check on the bawling child.

"Mrs. Pitovsky is sick, Peter," she called after him, "and I will not abandon her!" Having said this, Isabel escaped to her room.

She wondered for a moment how Jesus and some Lutherans ever met. At times it seemed they had so little in common. Was this the same Jesus who took time out for sick people, who made friends with sinners? It was hard for Isabel to understand how the Lutherans in her town could talk so much about Jesus, yet care so little about the things He stood for. It was as if they were only out to make new converts so they could then join the church and repeat the catechism, and its true meaning didn't much matter.

Turning back her bed, Isabel crawled in between the layers to rest. As she lay there looking up, she whispered, "Lord, if you want me to help poor Mrs. Pitovsky, please don't let it rain one drop tonight. Amen."

When Isabel got up the next morning she could see there wasn't so much as dew on the ground. She watched as the sun rose bright and clear and then knew what God wanted her to do. Peter would never understand. She barely understood it herself.

As soon as the early milking was finished, Isabel put on her Sunday dress and climbed into the dairy truck. She drove directly to the church, taking the pastor by surprise in her unabashed plea to get help for Helena.

"Izzy," Reverend Stoltzfus said, "I'm sorry, but there are too many in our own parish who are needy right now to take up the cause of those outside we don't even know."

"Yes, but God knows them. They're as dear to Him as any of those in our church. 'We can't shut up the bowels of our compassion toward the poor.'" It was an odd-sounding proverb but was somewhere in the King James Bible, and the pastor knew it.

"Are they Lutherans?" he asked.

"No, only hurting human beings ... Baptist, if anything," she added.

"Baptists? Izzy, Peter told me you've introduced strife into your family by allowing these vagrants to stay on your dairy farm. And while the plight of the poor is important, it's also important to keep peace at home."

"The Book of Deuteronomy says we're to show hospitality to the strangers in our midst," Isabel said. "That's all I'm doing. Our old dairyman's shed was empty and of no use to anyone. The Pitovsky family was sleeping in a junkyard. Their freezing in a dirty car like that couldn't have made much sense to the good Lord, because it sure didn't make any sense to me. Which is why I moved them into the empty shack. I had to do the simple thing and try to act like the Lord intended. I respect Peter because he's my brother, but Helena's very ill and she needs me. If she can't turn to the good people of God, who else will help her? 'Where kindness is greatest, there stands the throne of God.'" *Where have I heard that before?* she wondered.

"But, Izzy, this woman's not one of ours!" The pastor was almost shouting now.

"She's one of His! 'Do not shut up thy bowels of compassion against the needy.'" Isabel repeated the verse she'd used earlier. She wanted to cite where it was in the Bible but now wasn't sure it was in fact from there.

"The Bible also says before you offer your gift at the altar, you must first go home and be reconciled to your brother. Then come and offer your gift. When you've got things right with your family, maybe you'll be able to make things right with God."

" 'What doth the Lord require of thee but to do justice and love mercy,' " Isabel cried. "It's in Micah!"

" 'Rebuke not an older man, but treat him lovingly as a father,' " answered Reverend Stoltzfus. "It's from the Epistles."

" 'I was hungry and ye gave me no meat, thirsty and ye gave me no drink, naked and ye clothed me not, sick and ye ministered not to me!' " Isabel yelled back.

" 'The poor you have with you always!' "

Isabel and the pastor continued lobbing Scriptures at each other like hand grenades, returning volley for volley, when Isabel suddenly held her tongue. With tears trickling down her cheeks, she quickly gathered her things and ran for the door. Reverend Stoltzfus followed her, and her last sight of the pastor was his tall silhouette filling the doorway of the church.

But she didn't waste time forming a grudge. She waved at him from the window of the dairy truck, wishing he were a better man, then sped down the street.

Isabel could put out of her mind what happened with Reverend Stoltzfus. She couldn't stop thinking, however, about finding help for Helena. But help cost money. There was only one answer. Isabel had been reluctant to consider it, but now things were desperate and she felt she had no other choice. *Lord, please forgive me for what I'm about to do. I know you will. But, Lord, help Peter also to forgive me—he'll need your help with this. Lord, if what I'm going to do is not your will, please send me some sign that tells me so.* Isabel drove on to the bank quite certain of her mission. Then she'd catch the ten-thirty train into Philadelphia.

❧❧❧

Sometimes two momentous miracles take place within a single moment. As Isabel was hurrying out of the bank, Ingrid Mueller was walking in.

"Well, good morning Izzy," Ingrid said. "It's a beautiful day! Not much wind—a nice turn for March."

"There's a bit of wind in the east," Isabel replied. "A good day for miracles."

It was a strange statement, but Ingrid had known Isabel long enough not to give it another thought. "How's your new hired hand working out?"

"He's fine. His wife, Helena, could use some help, though. Still, God's got good things in store when the wind is right. This morning when I woke up and saw that rooster crowin' to the east, I knew it'd be a good day."

"What rooster?" Ingrid asked, then wished she hadn't. There was usually a kind of skewed logic connected with Isabel's thinking and often too convoluted to figure out on the spot, say, while standing with her in front of the bank.

"The rooster on our weather vane. When he

crows east—and he doesn't do it all that often—the wind's just right for the Almighty to do good things, like in Exodus." It seemed she was about to say good-bye, when she took Ingrid's gloved hand in her own. "Your Otto writes beautifully, Ingrid. Best stuff—next to the Bible—I've ever read. But better than its beauty is its wisdom." She now moved in close, which startled Ingrid. Isabel McCaslin at close range could be rather unnerving.

"I . . . I . . . well, I think so myself, Izzy. Where Otto got the ability, this gift of being able to write, I'm not sure. He's always kept so to himself, but when he gets alone the angels must sing."

"Indeed they must," agreed Isabel. "Mrs. Mueller, I've always been a pretty intense person and sometimes I feel so fidgety on the inside I can't do nothing but talk loud and quote Scripture. You know what I mean?"

Ingrid nodded, though she wasn't exactly sure.

"But when I read Otto's poetry, that intensity just sort of leaves me. It makes me wanna get quiet and be by myself, to see all the good things in life. It's then that I don't feel so crazy inside."

Ingrid now understood. And she knew a wonderful thing had occurred. For the first time in her life she was having a real conversation with Isabel McCaslin. How funny that it should happen here on the sidewalk in front of the bank and not in some fine teahouse, where two ladies might quietly find friendship in more elegant surroundings.

"Izzy, I wonder if you've got some of Otto's writings I've never read. I don't want to pry, but I'd so much like to see what you have."

"And I'd so much like to see what you have. Otto must have boxes of stuff I've never read. I know I'd be the better for it."

"Do you suppose we could have lunch sometime—at my place, of course—and then read each other's mail?" Ingrid could hardly believe she'd just welcomed "Dizzy Izzy" into her home. But she knew she hadn't welcomed Izzy, she'd invited *Isabel*. Suddenly she was inclined to believe Isabel and what she had said about the east wind. Might it also blow peace into a troubled mind? Perhaps the east wind was Otto's wind too. Ingrid could see that Isabel was changing. Had her Otto been a part of Isabel's healing, of her becoming a new person?

"The whole idea is delicious," Isabel said, interrupting Ingrid's reverie. "Let's do it. I . . . mean if you could find the time for it."

"Yes, of course. But we must be secret about this. It'll be our own private party to savor Otto's creativity. Agreed?"

Isabel agreed and then let go of Ingrid's hand.

Ingrid was almost sorry she did. For a moment, the touch of something wonderful had been hand in hand with her. And good things happen when two people touch in agreement.

"Good day, Ingrid," Isabel said as she whirled around and strode away toward the railroad station.

Even the way she said "Good day" was different somehow. Ingrid's encounter with Isabel served as a reminder that the impossible can happen. Their meeting symbolized that it's possible for the troubled of spirit, or mind even, to wake up and suddenly find themselves mended, made whole by the coming of truth.

She watched Isabel now as she headed for the train station. But why was she boarding the train? Ingrid planned to catch the ten-thirty herself in a few minutes. Was it possible they'd be riding the same coach? She knew the heaviness of her own business at the bank and wondered about Isabel's visit. What was it that Isabel held in her other hand? Was she on her way to Philadelphia or New York? And for what purpose?

It seems during their pleasant exchange on the sidewalk each of them had found a way to hide the burdens the world had laid on their courageous shoulders.

Ingrid found Isabel sitting alone in the third car just as the train was lurching away from the platform. "Isabel?" she said, in a tone that made it seem she'd just discovered her by accident.

"Mrs. Mueller!" Isabel was honestly surprised.

"Please, call me *Ingrid—Miss McCaslin.*"

They both laughed.

Ingrid's skirt was so full that when she went to sit down next to Isabel, her garment overlapped Isabel. She attempted to shove the folds to her side of the seat and tuck them under her but was having little success. There was just too much dress to make it work. Because the seat facing them was free, Ingrid rose and sat down opposite Isabel. "This is much better, anyway," Ingrid said. "Unless the coach fills up, we'll be able to talk better this way. You don't mind if I sit here, do you?"

"Of course not. I'm absolutely flattered. Are you traveling to Philadelphia or all the way to New York? Oh, I hope I'm not prying . . . forgive me."

"Nothing to forgive, dear. I'll be going on to New York. How about yourself?"

"Philadelphia is far enough for me."

"You don't have family there, do you?" Ingrid asked, then instantly she felt like a snoop again.

"No. Do you have family in New York?"

Ingrid shook her head. Then both women took a break from their gentle prying and settled back into their overstuffed seats. Gazing out the large window between them, they watched as the outskirts of King of Prussia flashed by their railcar.

After a while, however, Ingrid couldn't resist any longer. "Isabel, why are you going to Philadelphia?"

"Mrs. Mueller... I'm sorry, I mean, Ingrid, are there some things that are right, even when they appear wrong to other people? I've been trying to help the Pitovsky family, but Peter and even Reverend Stoltzfus think I'm doing the wrong thing."

"The Pitovskys?"

"They're the family who've been staying at our farm in the dairyman's shed. I hired Mr. Pitovsky, Ernest, to work at the dairy. But his wife, Helena, has consumption. Dr. Drummond says she probably won't live much longer unless she gets proper treatment at a sanatorium. The Reser Sanatorium in Philadelphia is the only affordable facility that can help her, although even they're expensive. I feel it's my duty to help Helena—I can't just let her die—but I can't find help anywhere. I've tried going to my family and our church. Nothing. Money's so tight. I can't think of any other way to raise the money but this." Isabel then reached inside her purse and pulled out a purple velvet drawstring pouch. Opening the small bag, she slowly lifted out the dazzling brooch.

"Are those diamonds real?" Ingrid asked, overwhelmed by the rainbow of light they reflected as Isabel held it in the sunlight now pouring through the coach's window.

"Yes. After the reading of Papa's will, I had it appraised at more than a thousand dollars. It was left to me, but I've decided to sell it and use the money for something good—four months worth of treatment for Helena at the sanatorium."

"Oh, Isabel, are you sure you're doing the right thing? This brooch must have meant a lot to your mother."

"It did. It's been in the family for generations. But I can't stand by and do nothing. I can't allow a friend to suffer and maybe die when this piece of jewelry could possibly save her. Am I crazy? The whole town seems to think so. Be honest and I'll accept what you say as the truth."

"Isabel, you're not crazy. Sometimes our doing what's right just makes us *look* crazy. I have a confession of my own." Ingrid unsnapped her handbag and drew out an envelope, which appeared to contain about two thousand dollars in cash.

Isabel gasped. "I don't think I've ever seen a hundred-dollar bill before, let alone fifteen or twenty of 'em! Why so much money?"

"Because Otto has a child!" Ingrid blurted it out not so much because she lacked tact, but because she wanted to see Isabel's reaction. It was a sort of test to gauge Isabel and Otto's relationship, how deeply the two felt about each other. Ingrid's suspicions were instantly confirmed.

"Otto has a child?" Isabel stared at her wide-eyed, looking as if a knife had been thrust into her heart.

"Yes ... well, she's not actually his child. Less than a year ago Otto befriended a dying woman whose young daughter, after her death, was kept by the same hospital-orphanage where the woman had died. The child is still there, and Otto's been miserable about it because the little girl's so unhappy. The problem is the late mother's remaining medical bills and the expenses at the orphanage, which Otto's been struggling to pay.

"But we've talked it over now as a family and decided we'd all do what we could to help, and to see a lawyer about seeking guardianship of the girl. I know the good people at church probably won't understand when we show up with a new family member out of nowhere. But right is right, don't you think? I've all but emptied our savings to make this possible. So am *I* crazy? Oh, why couldn't my boys have married their high-school sweethearts and had children? It would've been much easier explaining things to our church friends!"

The remark bothered Isabel, for she could see

that her own feelings for Otto may be threatening Ingrid's idea of who and how her sons should marry.

"At least you have friends," Isabel said. "I've never had to explain myself. . . . The town gossip has pretty much prevented me from forming any real relationships. You see, I've never been accepted as you are. And my 'Dizzy-Izzy' reputation isn't going to get any better when word gets around what I'm doing today."

"Isabel, if you ever need someone to sit with in church, you can sit with me. I'd consider it an honor." Ingrid leaned over and patted her hand.

They both turned to look out the coach window and were soon mesmerized by the flying telephone poles. Their knifelike shadows flickered through the glass, producing a hypnotic effect that kept the two women busy in the deep recesses of their minds.

Several minutes later Isabel pulled from her purse some of Otto's poems. Holding the pages out, she said, "Ingrid, see what I have here!"

Ingrid smiled weakly. She had no idea that Otto had given so much to Isabel. It was hard not to be offended by all Isabel had received from him, when she'd received so little. Ingrid nodded a curt thank-you and began reading. Once again, she felt she was witnessing the beginnings of a great poet. "Listen to this," Ingrid said.

"Ruth is born anew!
I've seen the Moabitess gleaning in the gold.

I've touched the harvesters
And bid them, let a little grain fall
For that strange, strange woman
Who is hungry for God's better bread.
I long for midnight,
For its promises of sweet togetherness,
Will give love force enough to heal a man's weak
limb
And better gild the face reflected in the soul's dark
glass."

Isabel sat silently as she contemplated the words of the poem. *Otto.* He'd come to her like some kind of lord yet unsure of his nobility. Then he set about serving and loving those who hungered for something better.

Ingrid continued flipping through the many pages in her hands. As they were nearing the Philadelphia station and the train began slowing down, she gasped, "Isabel, listen!

"Saints were never those
Who thought their service Godlike.
Saints loved and drifted fireward moth-to-flame.
Never noticing that they'd been set afire
Because they hungered to know God.
At last they found him
Living in the ordinary wounds
Of those they went to heal.
Saints are passion lepers who dared
to touch contagion.
And found themselves made whole.

Weeping is the only way to serve the weeping."

"It was that poem," Isabel said, "that fixed my desire to help the Pitovsky family. From that point on, I couldn't go back."

Suddenly Ingrid's eyes lit up. "How much do you trust me?" she asked. Isabel showed a quizzical look as their heads fell closer together. Soon they'd struck a bargain and were laughing out loud. The train then came to a full stop.

They switched some things between each of their purses, then stood up to hug each other good-bye. A moment later Isabel had stepped off the train, while Ingrid returned to her seat to prepare herself for the long trip to New York.

As the train pulled out of the station, Ingrid wondered which step to take next. But she wasn't disheartened. After all, the wind was in the east.

"It's der confounded *cow people* who von't pay der bills!"

Hans was as mad as Otto had ever seen him. Even the acute pain in his back didn't keep him from doubling up his fist and shaking it toward the sky.

Otto had just come in from the coal run. He feared approaching Hans when he was in such a mood, yet felt compelled to ask, "What's the matter, Papa?"

Hans laid a stack of papers back on his desk. He was obviously reviewing his accounts and brooding over what he referred to as "the unlucky streak of varm veather."

"Der matter? I'll tell you vhat's der matter. The cow people owe us seventy-eight dollars and dey von't pay up! Otto, vould you run out there after dinner tonight and tell 'em they're behind three deliveries on their account?"

"Sure, Papa."

"You may vant to take along some brass knuckles! Dem Scots keep their money in their kilts and they von't give it up mittout a little persuadin'. You tell him der cows are gonna get pretty cold if dey decide not to pay. Their udders will be frostbitten before he gets any more coal from us!"

Otto knew that, whatever his tactic, he'd probably not mention frostbitten udders. Since Ingrid wasn't home, Otto quickly made himself a jelly sandwich and munched it with a tall glass of McCaslin milk. While he drank he couldn't help thinking of the possible frozen udders out at the McCaslin Dairy.

Before long Otto was in the truck, heading for the dairy farm. When he got there he discovered that the man of the house wasn't at home. *Rotten luck*, he thought. Peter was at his lodge meeting. But Isabel was there, although she couldn't write him a check.

It turned out, however, that Isabel volunteered to pay the entire bill in cash, in exchange for a receipt that indicated the balance was now zero.

Otto wondered if Isabel had gotten Peter's permission to pay the coal bill out of his cash box. While most businesses their size settled their accounts using bank drafts, Peter preferred cash. Some said Peter's "cash-and-carry" dairy business left fewer records for the tax people to figure out just how much money he really made.

Otto placed the money inside a zippered leather wallet.

After finishing the business of the overdue coal bill, Isabel looked up at Otto and said, "I just opened a Mason jar of peaches. Want some?" Actually Isabel hadn't yet opened the jar, but she would in a heartbeat if she saw the slightest glimmer of approval in Otto's eyes.

"Sounds great," Otto said.

"I also have a quart of sugared cream on ice!" she exclaimed.

"Well, bring it on!" he said, smiling at Isabel's overenthusiastic offer. "You sure it won't be any trouble?"

" 'Trouble?' said the spider to the fly."

It was such an utterly human response and so unlike the tangled and distant Isabel that Otto once knew. He let out a hearty laugh.

"Can I take your coat, Otto?"

He handed it over.

"Oh, it's all coaly," she grimaced.

"It's how I make my living, how I collect my overdue bills." He caught her eye and smiled.

Isabel made coffee and, while it was brewing, set out a large bowl of peaches drenched in golden sugared cream.

"This is decadent," Otto said. "Should we be doing this? I mean, think of the starving people in China."

"Forget the Chinese! It takes eight weeks to get

there on a steamer. How could we ever get it to 'em before it spoiled?" she asked as she placed the coffee cups on the table. "Otto, enjoy it! A treat like this doesn't come very often these days."

They talked long after the peaches and cream were gone. Otto noticed that Isabel's tendency to quote Scripture, to punctuate her end of the conversation, had greatly diminished.

"Otto, you've brought some things to this town—to my world—that never existed before."

"You mean like stealing Mabel's coal scoop and making you think I'd bought it for you?"

"That was a mistake."

"I'm not sure Mabel thinks so."

"But I'm talking about your poetry. The stuff you write is incredibly good." She paused and then asked, "You did bring me something to read, didn't you?"

He nodded. "You can't have it till I leave, though."

It turned out to be the perfect evening. Peter stayed late at the lodge, and Kathleen and the baby never intruded. At first their time together was flanked with propriety as they sat on the small settee and talked. Then it seemed the arms of the small sofa closed in on them, pushing them closer together—closer than propriety might dictate. Isabel turned her face toward his and then . . . then the angels sang.

"It's getting late," Otto said. "I'd best go. Still, I

agree with Romeo when he said, 'I have more of a will to stay than to go, but I must go.' "

The two stood together. They were suddenly caught up in a long embrace that finally ended when Otto broke away and went for the door.

Isabel followed after him. "Don't forget your coaly coat," she called.

He snapped it up, gave her a wide grin, then said good-night.

" 'Oh, wilt thou leave me so unsatisfied?' " she said.

Otto was pleased she too knew a line or two from *Romeo and Juliet*.

Then the rumble of tires filled their ears. Looking out in the yard, they saw Peter turning onto the gravel driveway.

Their ardor died instantly.

It seemed to Isabel that Peter had a way of killing everything warm and lovely.

Otto tipped his hat to propriety and only kissed her hand, saying his good-night again. It was a gallant ending, which Peter witnessed as he passed them on the porch and entered the house. He had glared at Isabel, who was still aglow from the peaches-and-cream drama that Peter hadn't seen.

Otto and Isabel parted hands, and then before she knew it, he was driving away from the farm in the coal truck.

Isabel felt her pocket. Otto had slipped a folded piece of paper into it. She walked into the house, poured herself a fresh cup of coffee, and hurried to her room.

When Isabel had locked her door, she unfolded the slip of paper. Now the party was hers alone. She picked up her coffee and took a sip, then started to read.

> *There are wondrous forks*
> *In every route to happiness*
> *And those who face such grand division,*
> *Hold life together,*
> *Refusing to be separate, they know*
> *That either road beyond*
> *The fork is right.*
> *The issue never was "which road?"*
> *But "Will we walk together?"*
> *For the destination never is the point.*
> *All that matters is the journey.*

Isabel hesitated as she sipped at the coffee. She read Otto's name over and over again, marveling at how it appeared. He was her own dear courtier.

After his name, Otto had written, "Canticles 8:7: 'Many waters cannot quench love, neither can the floods drown it.'"

14

The Friday exactly two weeks before Good Friday arrived wet and cold. Isabel knew early on that, while it wasn't Good Friday yet, it would be an extraordinary Friday nonetheless. For this is the day Helena checked into Reser Sanatorium at nine in the morning, and by three that afternoon, Otto and Marguerite LeBlanc had been met by Hans at the railroad station. The day marked the beginnings of a significant shift in the lives of two families.

Now the Pitovsky children clung to Isabel, while the somewhat frightened Marguerite clung to Otto. Hans would've taken to Marguerite right away, except that the child shrunk back in fear when he extended his beefy hand to her. Otto's bedroom was sufficiently large to hold the extra bed, and given the child's insecurities, the family felt it was the best of all possible arrangements.

The Pitovsky children were quite another matter. They'd been so brutalized by their living in the cold, their mother's warmth had become the only safe haven of their world. Obviously Isabel was unable to supply them with the same kind of security. And although Ernest tried to stay with them as much as possible, he felt he had to continue with his work at the dairy, to support his family as best he could. Further, Ernest knew his presence on the farm had created a lot of tension between Isabel and her brother; therefore, he wished to be the best employee they had, to prove to Peter, hopefully, his worthiness to stay on and work there long-term.

One morning Ernest asked Isabel to watch the children when he wasn't working. He'd already finished his early-morning shift. Thinking he just needed a little time to himself, Isabel agreed without hesitation. She had no idea what Ernest was up to or she would've stopped him. So after their grueling breakfast, Isabel was entertaining Freiderich and Katrinka in the dairyman's shack, while Ernest carried out his plan.

He'd decided that he would walk over to the "big house," as his children called it, and make a call on Peter. So a little after ten o'clock, not knowing how he was about to complicate things, Ernest knocked on the front door of the McCaslin home.

Kathleen managed to swing open the door while holding the baby. She'd never met Ernest and for a moment couldn't figure out the identity of the man now standing on her porch. She only saw that he was poorly dressed and that he looked cold and bedraggled.

"Howdy, ma'am. My name's Ernest Pitovsky. I work here in the dairy."

"Um . . . yes, Ernest, I've heard Peter and Izzy speak of you." Kathleen's words were very much an understatement. She'd often heard them shouting Ernest's name at each other since his first showing up at the dairy farm.

"I was wondering if Peter is in," Ernest said.

"I'll get him. Come in and have a seat."

"Thank you." He entered the home and the first thing that caught his eye was the magnificent crystal chandelier hanging in the foyer that shone brilliantly in spite of the dull light trickling in from the gray day. Ernest took a seat in an upholstered armchair but was reluctant to lean back, fearing he might get it dirty. He couldn't help but notice the extreme contrast between the fine furnishings of the house he now sat in and the plainness of the dairyman's shed. He felt wrong in the place and suddenly wished he'd waited outside on the porch. Then when Mr. McCaslin appeared, he would've been able to speak his piece more comfortably—outside the "big house." While Ernest was lost in a rising cloud of self-doubt, Peter strode into the room. Ernest quickly jumped to his feet.

"No, please, keep your seat!" Peter said in an unusually nice voice.

His warm demeanor threw Ernest off guard. He sat back down in the expensive winged chair, though still sitting stiffly forward so as not to touch more of it than was necessary.

"Now, what can I do for you?" Peter asked. His tone had dropped the warmth of his initial greeting and turned suddenly more intense, more business-like.

"Well, sir, I felt I should come here and say thank you."

"You can thank my sister for the job. She feels we otta hire people like you, and I ... well, I don't. You can have the job for a while, but probably only for a while."

"Sir, I'm grateful for the job and you need to know that. And I'd feel less than grateful if I didn't say thank you." Ernest was mustering all the courage he had to talk to Peter, and Peter's way of speaking wasn't making it easy.

"Like I said, if there's any thanks to be given, Izzy's the one that otta be thanked."

Ernest straightened himself in the already too-straight chair as if his mind was having to convince his backbone to say the rest of what he'd come to say.

"Yes ... well, sir, living in the open fields this winter was very hard, especially on Helena and the children. I can't tell you how my wife has suffered. Dr. Drummond said she wouldn't make it if she didn't get treatment at a sanatorium. When I found out that you folks had arranged for her treatment, I'm not a praying man, but I got on my knees and thanked God. Mr. McCaslin, I don't reckon that without my wife I'd find much of a reason for living. I don't know how I'll ever make it up to you, but so help me God, I'll find some way."

During Ernest's speech, Peter's face had drained of all color, then turned a bright red. His hands drew into fists, his knuckles whitened. "What! Are you telling me your wife's been admitted to a sanatorium and it's McCaslin money that's paying for it? I don't believe this!"

"Um . . . sir, I'm sorry . . . but I thought you knew!" Ernest stammered.

With a scowl spreading across his face, Peter moved in closer to Ernest, who remained sitting in the chair. He stood over him and pointed his finger at Ernest's nose. "You people are leeches! Don't you realize this is the Depression? Get out of here. YOU'RE FIRED!"

Ernest was trembling now. When he went to stand up and leave he couldn't avoid bumping into Peter, who was still planted in front of the chair. Peter shoved him back down, causing Ernest's weight to hit the chair at an odd angle and with such force that the chair tipped over on its side and spilled Ernest onto the floor. An end table and antique lamp had also gotten knocked over in all the commotion. The lamp slammed against the wall, then shattered on the floor. To make matters worse, Ernest had cut his hand rather severely on the broken glass as he was scrambling to get up off the floor and then dripped blood on the carpet.

"Now get off my farm, you clumsy ox!" Peter shouted.

Holding his injured hand tight against his chest with his good hand, Ernest ran for the door and got himself out onto the porch. He stopped and struggled to take a deep breath, feeling sick to his stomach and ashamed that he had broken the lamp and angered Peter. More than anything, though, he was ashamed he'd lost his job. He didn't know what to do. He was thankful now that he'd managed to save almost a month's wages in a coffee can back at the dairyman's shed. He wrapped his hand in his shirttail and walked as fast as he could away from the house.

When he reached the shack, Isabel, seeing the dazed look in his eyes and his blood-soaked hand, was bewildered as to what could've caused such a thing. "What in the world! Ernest, what happened?"

"Oh, Miss Isabel, I'm so sorry. I've made a mess of things. I wanted to thank Peter for his help in taking care of my Helena. But he didn't know anything about her being at the sanatorium. He became very upset and then he fired me."

"He did what?"

"He ordered me to get off the place at once." Ernest was shaking again.

"Well, Peter can't do that! I own half of this farm."

"Please, Miss Isabel, I don't want to cause any

more problems in the family. I've already caused enough trouble."

"You haven't caused any trouble, Ernest. You're a hard worker and good dairyman and you don't have to leave. I'm gonna go to the house right now and have it out with him. Peter's got a mean streak, and I've tried to work around it, but I'm through bein' nice. You and the children just stay put and I'll be back as soon as I can." Isabel hurried out the door and started running down the path toward the house.

Ernest didn't listen to her. As much as he wanted to stay, he felt unwelcome and that it would be best for everyone that he move on. Ernest wasted no time. He tied his things up in a bundle and dressed the children.

"Where we goin', Papa?" asked Freiderich.

"First, we're gonna go see Mama and we'll figure the rest out from there." But Ernest didn't mean "go see Mama," he meant "go *get* Mama." He was sure his hopes for Helena's treatment were now dashed. And their dreams of making a new start in life were maybe forever dashed as well. Slinging his bundle of goods over his shoulder, Ernest scooped up Katrinka and took Freiderich by the hand, and then the three of them stepped out into the morning.

Though the east wind had all but died, at least the rain had stopped. Clinging to one another, the Pitovsky family was again on the move. They seemed to be in exodus, perpetually in exodus, and always walking somewhere, anywhere. Maybe if they walked fast enough, far enough, their world would change and their situation improve. This time they walked toward King of Prussia to look for the railroad station. All Ernest knew was that he had more money in his pocket walking out of the McCaslin Dairy than he had when he'd walked in. Now they could ride the train into Philadelphia instead of having to walk the tracks. But even if he had a little cash, Ernest could still sense it would be a hard day, like the many exhausting days before.

❧

"Peter McCaslin, you're a disgrace to everything human!"

"Never mind that. Izzy, how did you pay for that woman's hospitalization costs?"

"That's none of your business! Now, I want you to do the first decent thing you've done in quite a while. I want you to go out to the shack and apologize to Ernest. He's devastated."

"I'm sorry . . . sorry because he's an ignorant drifter who you gave a lot of false hope to. Besides, he's no worse off now than he was before he came here."

"You mean when he was living in a junkyard down by the railroad trestle?"

"Yeah, I guess. There's a lot of people having it rough these days, Izzy. You can't save the whole lousy world! Answer my question, where did you get the money for that woman to be hospitalized?"

"I've got my ways. You go apologize to Mr. Pitovsky! He's in tremendous need right now. You've humiliated a good man!"

"Like I said, he's in no greater need than before you first began pumping his head full of false hope by letting him move into our shed. And just how did you come up with the kind of money it takes to pay for someone to get treated at a sanatorium in Philadelphia? You better not have sold or mortgaged anything to do with my farm! Well, did you?"

In a show of indifference, Isabel turned her back on Peter and started out of the room. But Peter clutched her elbow and spun her back around.

"Peter, stop it! You're hurting me!"

Isabel's screaming had alerted Kathleen, who came rushing in from the baby's room at the back of the house. "What's going on out here?" she said.

"Ouch! Let go of me, Peter!" Isabel tried to wriggle out of his grasp, but he'd tightened his hold on her upper arms till it felt his fingernails were about to draw blood. Isabel's efforts to free herself failed, so she went limp and whimpered in his direction, "You're evil, Peter." It wasn't much of a rebuke.

Then the back of Peter's hand caught her brutally in the face. He'd hit her much harder than he intended, but this was something he realized only afterward when it was too late. Isabel pitched backward as blood spurted from her nose and lip. He let her go and she fell the rest of the way to the floor.

Isabel then looked up at him and, in between sobs, said, " 'Be ye kind . . . one to another . . . tender-hearted, forgiving one another . . . even as God for Christ's sake has forgiven you!' "

"Dizzy Izzy! The town loony and religious weirdo. Get out!" Peter was about to kick her in the side as she attempted to get up, when Kathleen grabbed his arm and pulled him back.

"Peter, stop it! Get ahold of yourself," Kathleen shouted.

Still crying, Isabel slowly got to her feet. She pulled out her handkerchief and blotted the blood from her nose and mouth. "This is my house too! I don't have to get out," she said through her tears.

He started toward her once again, so she decided that, her house or not, she'd better leave for a while. Isabel staggered out to the porch and then into the open air, relieved to be away from Peter's anger. She'd seen him mad before but not to the point of striking her.

Isabel didn't return to the dairyman's shed right away. Instead she walked the fence line to recover her bearings. She continued to dab at her wounds while walking and thinking till finally coming to the junkyard where she'd first seen the Pitovskys. She wondered how she could ever help someone like Peter to see there was another world out there, a world where life was reduced to survival. The good Lord alone must know what Ernest thought of the McCaslins now.

She felt if she could just talk to Otto or Ingrid, things would look better. It was this thought that turned her back toward the farm. Maybe Ingrid would help. Or Otto. But unfortunately for Isabel, the worst of her day hadn't yet come. This happened a little later, when she entered the dairyman's shed and found it empty.

15

"Ingrid, Ingrid!" called Isabel as she pounded on the door.

Ingrid ran to the front of her house as fast as she could. When she opened the door, she saw Isabel was excited and out of breath. The old dairy truck was parked on an angle in the driveway behind her.

"Isabel? Come in, please. Is anything wrong?" Then noticing that her face was bruised and her upper lip cut and swollen, Ingrid blurted, "Oh, Isabel! What happened?"

Isabel didn't want to rehash the issue of Peter's meanness. There were more important things on her mind. "Ingrid, my brother fired Ernest, and now he and the children are gone! I told him to stay in the shed till I got back from talking to Peter, but he must've decided he was too much trouble for us and then left. I'm not sure where they've gone, but I know he had a little money saved and so probably took the train to the city. I'm almost sure he intends to take Helena out of Reser Sanatorium. I'm going to the city now, driving the dairy truck. Could you possibly go with me?"

Ingrid scribbled a note to Hans, and the two women soon found themselves speeding along the narrow two-lane highway that led to Philadelphia. Isabel figured Ernest had a four-hour head start and might already have reached the city and checked Helena out of Reser's. During the ride, Isabel told Ingrid about her terrible fight with Peter and how angry he'd become. She could only imagine all the hate-filled invectives he had aimed at Ernest.

"Peter asked me repeatedly how I'd paid the sanatorium bill."

"You didn't tell him our secret, did you?" Ingrid asked.

"No, I didn't. My life is my life, Ingrid. And Peter can't go on tellin' me he's got some special claim on the dairy because I'm crazy."

"Did he say that?"

Isabel nodded, keeping her eyes fixed on the road ahead.

"Dear Isabel! 'Beware Alexander the Coppersmith, who did me great evil. He who is angry at his brother without a cause shall have his part in the Lake of Fire.'" Now Ingrid was quoting Scripture.

"Oh, Ingrid, that's too stern! Quote no more Scripture. Even Peter deserves something better than that."

"Yes, I suppose so. Still, your brother's as mean

as those snakes that fled before John the Baptist's fire."

"Ingrid, please, no more Scripture. You'll get yourself all lopsided, like I used to be."

Ingrid knew Isabel was right, so she practiced settling down as the dairy truck rattled on toward town. And by the time she was fully at peace, they were pulling up in front of Reser's. They hurried inside just in time to see the lanky form of a man with two little children proceeding down the hall before them.

"Ernest!" yelled Isabel in a voice so urgent and loud it didn't fit at all in the hospital's quiet hallways.

Ernest wheeled around. "Oh, Miss Isabel ... I'm sorry, but I had to leave. I was causing terrible strife in your family."

"No, that's not true! There's always been strife in my family. You just brought it to the surface. My papa left the dairy to both me and Peter, but Peter just doesn't want to honor that. But it's still half mine. He sees me as incompetent and crazy and he sees you as riffraff. The truth is that the strife's all in Peter. Ernest, you haven't checked Helena out, have you?"

"No, Miss Isabel. Not yet. We just got here."

"Please, Ernest, Helena's bill has been paid to cover four months of treatment. I want Helena to get well and of course so do you and the children, and I believe that God wants her to get well too. So

I propose we all go visit her and then all go back home. It's my home. It's your home. It's where you work. Just stay away from Peter, and I promise you he'll give you no more trouble. I've taken care of Peter. He doesn't know it yet, but he's about to like both of us a lot less but treat us a lot better. But for the time being, let's go see Helena."

At the mention of their mother's name, Freiderich and Katrinka turned suddenly ecstatic, shouting, "Hooray, hooray, hooray!" They each put their little hands in their father's and pulled him down the long corridor as they ran toward Helena's room.

Already Helena looked a little better since coming to the sanatorium, better than they'd imagined. She was less pale. Maybe it was the environment or maybe it was the new medicines she'd been taking— but she *did* look better.

Ingrid met the Pitovsky family for the first time that day and she was delighted by the power of their wholesome neediness and the spirit of their gratitude.

After they had all visited for about an hour, Ernest said, "Helena, I have to go now. There's the evening milking, you know. I'm getting good at it too. Never thought I would, but I am." He leaned over and kissed her, then he lifted Freiderich and Katrinka by turns, and they each kissed her as well.

Ingrid and Isabel waved a timid good-bye, almost feeling guilty for intruding on a family as sacred as the Pitovskys seemed to be.

They were just leaving the room when Helena raised herself on one elbow and called, "Isabel!" It was a weak call but surprisingly strong for her condition. Isabel turned and, along with Ingrid, retraced her steps back to the snow-white bed.

"Isabel, you know Ernest and I aren't very religious people, but I shudder to think what would've become of us if you hadn't found us and cared for us. No one else has ever done that. We had been to every welfare agency we heard about, and no one seemed to care. But you cared. You cannot know how much I think of you. I never found church people very loving, until I met you. Now I know that, somewhere in your good heart, there must be the God of good people. I want my children to grow up and be like you. Isabel, would you do me a favor and take my children to Sunday school with you this week, and every week, till I'm better and can do it myself?"

Ernest and the children had moved so that now they were standing right behind Isabel. Helena craned her neck a bit to make eye contact with Ernest, then said, "Ernest, it wouldn't hurt you any either." Ernest looked sheepish in that he had to be reminded.

"No," he agreed, "it wouldn't hurt me any either."

"And, Ernest, would you take a couple of dollars out of the coffee can and buy the children some new clothes, so they'll fit in with the other kids?"

"New shoes too?" Katrinka asked.

"That's right! New shoes. Ernest, will you?"

He nodded and then kissed her good-bye once again.

When they were all snuggled tightly in the dairy truck, Ernest looked over at Isabel. "Helena's right. I want our children to be like you, Isabel—minus the split lip, of course."

Everyone laughed.

Ernest then turned serious. "Miss Isabel, would you take my money and buy Freiderich and Katrinka a set of clothes and new shoes for Sunday school? I don't know much about how to pick out pretty stuff."

"Of course! I'd be happy to."

Ingrid fought a stinging in her eyes. She felt the simple pageants of life were often the best. And in her opinion, Isabel knew more than anyone how to direct a big show with a small cast of characters.

16

On Easter morning Peter McCaslin made sure the cows were milked a half hour early. Depression or not, Kathleen and the baby had new outfits to show off.

Isabel, on the other hand, had put fifteen cents worth of new ribbon on last year's dress, which she got new the Easter of '26. But then "extravagance was the bread of vanity," said Proverbs. Or did it? Maybe it said it, but not exactly that way. It was a verse she often quoted to herself before she got honest. *It may not be in the Book of Proverbs, but it otta be.*

She hated to spoil Peter's Easter, but she had something to show him before they all left for church. She was careful to go out and start the truck first, as she had every intention of driving to church alone. While the truck idled, Isabel walked back into the McCaslin parlor, where Peter and the baby were waiting for Kathleen.

Isabel knew that what she was about to do would be difficult and would put a damper on everyone's Easter holiday. It was something Peter wouldn't want to face. But she had to do it all the same. After removing a manila envelope from the center of her overly large Bible, she stepped over to Peter and said, "Peter, I went recently to Wolf's Studio and had my picture taken." Isabel didn't hand him the envelope for fear he might tear the photograph to pieces. Instead she pulled it out of the envelope and held it out for him to see.

The picture was a close-up of Isabel. She was looking straight into the camera lens with a bruised cheek, a black eye, and a puffy split lip. It had obviously been taken right after Peter hit her.

Peter tried to grab it, but Isabel was too quick for him. She'd picked her moment well: He was holding the baby as Kathleen finished putting on her new Easter fineries, so he was limited as to what he could do. Peter moved to block the front doorway. Isabel sprinted for the back. Seeing what she was up to, Peter ran to the front porch, the baby bouncing in his arms. But by the time Peter appeared, Isabel had already made it around the house and leaped into the dairy truck.

She backed it out, then drove straight to the dairyman's shed. Just then Ernest Pitovsky and the children emerged from the shack and quickly climbed into the front seat with her. Isabel turned onto the long driveway, shifting gears and sending gravel flying as they headed for the church.

In her rearview mirror, Isabel watched Peter

shrink in size and then finally disappear. It was a sign to Isabel. She had resolved that he would get even smaller in her determination to live her own life, to be her own person. *After all*, she thought, *"A man that striketh a woman, let him be an abomination throughout the land."* It was a Scripture she invented because she couldn't call to mind one that she needed. Then she smiled, squared her shoulders, stuck out her chin, and said to herself, *This is the day Jesus rose from the dead. Maybe it's time I did too.*

17

Mrs. Drummond and Kathleen McCaslin were both wearing new dresses. But that was all the new clothes to be seen, except, of course, for Freiderich and Katrinka. The church was already full when Peter walked in. Isabel had waited in the foyer for his arrival, and when he did show up, he smiled weakly at her. She looked him in the eye and smiled back, and for the first time in her life, she felt confident in his presence. Feeling renewed by a self-assurance she'd never known before, Isabel fell in behind Kathleen, who followed Peter in the McCaslin promenade to the second pew.

Ernest and the children sat at the back of the church. Peter gave them his look of disgust that said "riffraff." Ernest caught Peter's eye, quickly glanced to the side, and then ended up staring at the floor. It was clear Peter wished Ernest had gone to the Baptist church, where he would fit in.

But Freiderich and Katrinka had on their new clothes and shoes, which, although Peter didn't know it, Isabel had helped them to buy. So even to Peter's way of thinking, the children were as "Lutheran" as necessary.

Peter was as good at acting as he was at business. As he walked toward the front—where it got more and more crowded—Peter smiled at the Drummonds, feeling sorry that Mrs. Drummond, as nice as she was, was but a convert and not Lutheran-born. He passed Mabel Cartwright, noticing she wore the same serge dress as always. Peter reckoned she was as pretty as a sour Lutheran could make herself on Resurrection Sunday.

Finally, he proceeded past the "coal people." Erick was sitting next to Mary. *Lucky Mary*, as Peter thought of her. And then there was Otto, the crippled ne'er-do-well, who had begged his way back home after he'd lost it all on Wall Street.

Sitting beside Otto was a new little girl. Probably Otto's. Probably illegitimate. Who knew what he'd been up to during all those years he was away? He then glanced at Ingrid and Hans, the second-generation immigrants, who still talked with a funny accent from the country that started wars.

In spite of Isabel's earlier confrontation, Peter felt good about being Peter.

The McCaslin family now reached the second pew, and just as Peter was about to sit down, to his left he caught sight of Ingrid smiling serenely with a glitzy piece of paste jewelry on her collar. Peter froze.

154

It wasn't just glitzy paste jewelry. It was his late mother's diamond brooch, which was supposed to be in the safe-deposit box at the bank. So what was it doing on Ingrid Mueller's collar? "Oh no, Izzy!" Peter said. "What have you done?"

Peter scowled at his sister, who then smiled and pulled the manila envelope from her Bible. Again Peter tried to grab the envelope out of her hand, and again Isabel evaded his grasp as she stood up. There was nothing else to be done. Isabel stepped out into the center aisle of the church.

Then she did an odd thing. While the eyes of the congregation fell solidly on her, she strode to the rear of the church. Where was she going? Was she leaving before the Easter service had even begun?

On her way out of the church, she halted at the last pew and then sat down with Ernest and the children. They seemed honored that Isabel would walk back and sit by them.

Just like Izzy to go and sit with the riffraff! Peter fumed.

Isabel knew she'd done the right thing. When she passed Ernest earlier, she saw that he was fidgety, sitting alone, and poorly dressed. He was clearly new to the religious caste system.

Miss Isabel has come to sit with us, and in front of all these people! What a saint she is, Ernest thought. Now God felt real. And religion was maybe worthwhile after all. Ernest looked over at Isabel and realized he was somehow part of these people, no matter the pew they sat in, whether brushing the altar up front or way in the back. Isabel was as good a friend as anyone could possibly have, and he was a better man because of her friendship.

Then Otto and Marguerite rose and retraced the center aisle as though they too might leave. Like Isabel before them, they stopped at the last row and quietly sat down next to the Pitovsky family and Isabel. Except for them, the pew had been mostly empty. So there was enough room, although everyone had to slide over a bit.

Peter watched in disbelief as the whole social makeup of his Lutheran church became unglued before his eyes. He whispered to Kathleen that he'd be right back. He then got up and walked to the back. When he had reached the "Pitovsky pew," he said, "Izzy, your place is with us, up front."

Isabel shook her head, then glared at him as she tapped the manila envelope that stuck out of her Bible. Because Otto and Marguerite were sitting between Isabel and where Peter was standing, there was no way for Peter to make another attempt at getting the envelope. At least there wasn't any way while maintaining proper discretion. Peter didn't want anyone there to suspect he was less than the paragon of McCaslin virtue.

Therefore, he had no choice but to return to the front and once again take his seat by Kathleen.

The Muellers had watched the whole thing along with all the other astonished Lutherans.

Hans placed a firm hand on his back as he stood up to take part in the drama of the church's center aisle. "Come on, Ingrid. Ve should all sit together on Easter."

So Ingrid, and also Erick and Mary and Alexis, shuffled over to the Pitovsky pew. Of course, more wriggling and shifting was required to make room for everyone.

Peter saw them all as a sad bunch of refugees: a ragtag milker, coal people, a widow, and a cripple.

But they saw themselves as a newly formed family, drawn together by common need, and forged into oneness by one overarching fact—they sincerely loved one another.

Reverend Stoltzfus entered, and the church rose to sing "Alleluia! Christ Is Risen!" Ernest looked forward to the singing yet was unfamiliar with the hymn. But sometimes just wanting to sing is a song in itself. Freiderich and Katrinka had new clothes and new shoes, and that was the best kind of praise they could offer. The Muellers sang, and Mary Withers and Isabel sang. It was a good Easter, the season of miracles.

Isabel didn't need to be told what the weather was doing. It was all confirmed the moment she stepped out of church. There was a marvelous breeze. It was blowing to the east, or maybe southeast, but east enough to mean a miracle.

Far away in Philadelphia Helena Pitovsky lay in

her bed recovering. Yet she still felt herself to be part of their joy.

Peter would soon learn that Isabel had rented her own safe-deposit box at the bank. He knew he'd probably never get to see inside it. He wasn't exactly sure how Isabel had paid for Helena's medical treatment but surmised that her safe-deposit box held the answer. Did the coal people now own the family heirloom? Or had Isabel mortgaged the dairy trucks?

Ingrid never wore the brooch again, and Peter would never be certain what had become of it. Whether or not it ended up in Isabel's box at the bank would be something he'd never figure out. For Easter was the last time he'd ever see it. Ingrid and Isabel were friends now, and somewhere deep in their friendship—and deep inside the bank box— were secrets only they knew.

In the meantime, the wind warmed the land like the breath of God. Ingrid believed it was Isabel's great kindness that had lured the wind to warm all of eastern Pennsylvania.

Except for the Pitovskys, who would be going to the sanatorium for the day, all the others were invited to the Mueller house for Easter dinner.

But before they all split up for their various destinations, Hans surveyed the large company of "Muellers." He and Ingrid, Erick, Mary, Alexis, the three Pitovskys, and of course, Otto, Marguerite, and Isabel. Eleven of them in all.

"The wind feels good! God bless it!" Isabel said, interrupting Hans' thoughts as he exited the church. They were all outside in the churchyard when Isabel blessed the wind.

Ernest smiled. He had come to King of Prussia in search of hope and found it. Isabel could bless the wind if she wished, but Ernest knew it was much more than the wind. It was his day of fortune when Isabel McCaslin, this strange and wonderful woman, had walked into his life. The wind was blowing back then too.

"Happy Easter, Mr. Pitovsky," Isabel said. "How'd you like church?"

"Church was fine," Ernest admitted. "But any church where you went would be a good church. A place to hope. After all, hope is just catching a glimpse of the God of good people." Ernest blushed at hearing himself quote Isabel.

"Is that in the Bible?" Ingrid asked.

Isabel laughed. "No, but it otta be!"

Ernest didn't consider his words a benediction to Easter. They were more like an invocation for their life together. They could've been said by anyone who had come to believe God had taken up residence in Pennsylvania.

Who knew where life was going?

As Otto had written, life's destination is never the point. All that matters is the journey. For the moment there was light. Jesus was out of the tomb. The old bronze rooster was crowing to the east!